CALL THE ROSTER
OF THE HARD CORPS

WILLIAM O'NEAL — The baddest and the best. This one-time Green Beret captain picks the wars and calls the shots.

JAMES WENTWORTH III — Proud Oklahoman, well-rounded killer, master of the East's deadliest fighting arts.

JOE FANELLI — Street-corner wise guy turned demolitions expert, he's far more explosive than his beloved TNT.

STEVE CAINE — Silent lone wolf, who works behind enemy lines with blade, crossbow, and strangler's cord.

JOHN McSHAYNE — Top sergeant, master mechanic, and keeper of the incredible Hard Corps arsenal.

THE HARD CORPS

The HARD CORPS series from Jove

THE HARD CORPS
BEIRUT CONTRACT
WHITE HEAT
SLAVE TRADE (coming October 1987)

THE HARD CORPS

WHITE HEAT

CHUCK BAINBRIDGE

JOVE BOOKS, NEW YORK

WHITE HEAT

A Jove Book / published by arrangement with
the author

PRINTING HISTORY
Jove edition / July 1987

ISBN: 0-515-09083-2

Jove Books are published by The Berkley Publishing Group,
200 Madison Avenue, New York, NY 10016.
The words ''JOVE BOOKS'' and the ''J'' with logo
are trademarks belonging to Jove Publications, Inc.

Dedicated to
Melany Fritz
and
Colwyn Beckett

CHAPTER 1

THE INDIAN'S BODY convulsed wildly as high-velocity slugs crashed into his torso. Blood seeped from his woolen poncho as the man cried out and crumpled to the ground. Two gunmen approached the twitching form and sprayed another salvo of submachine-gun rounds into the dying glob of mangled flesh. It was overkill, of course, but the *coquitos* wanted to make an example of the Indian: a warning to others not to interfere in their clandestine business.

And they intended to make two more examples as well.

The three Indians had been following the river, hoping to find a suitable area for sugar cane in the region of Bolivia known as Las Yungas. Bolivia is a massive country, the fifth largest in South America, but with a population of less than six and a half million. Opportunities for claiming new land and developing resources and crops are plentiful. The three *indios* had not expected to come across a band of cocaine merchants in the process of purchasing 150 kilos of coca leaves, delivered by boat shortly before the Indians arrived.

The *coquitos* had just finished paying for the innocent-looking plastic bags of coca leaves. Four armed body-guards for the *coquito* lieutenant in charge scanned the

1

area with wary and suspicious eyes. When they saw the three unsuspecting Indians, the gunmen immediately opened fire with submachine guns. One *indio* was killed instantly while the other two bolted for the cover of the tall grass and ferns along the river edge.

The gangsters fired at the fleeing pair. Bullets slashed plants and split the stems of ferns as the Indians dived into the river. Water splashed from the descending figures. An Uzi submachine gun snarled, riddling the water's surface with 9-mm parabellum rounds. Arms and legs thrashed about wildly in the river as a dark stain spread from the struggling figure.

The victim's limbs ceased to move. The gunmen watched from the edge of the river as the shape bobbed into view. Long black hair drifted from a bullet-shattered skull. The dead man's poncho floated loosely from his lifeless frame. Arms hung wide apart across the water in an aquatic imitation of crucifixion.

The two eager gunmen waded knee deep in the water, searching for the first and last Indian. They shuffled through soft mud, holding their automatic weapons above the surface of the water. The pair cursed as water seeped into their shoes and through their trousers. They were products of the cities and uncomfortable in situations that took them beyond the comfort of concrete and steel.

"*Allá!*" a triggerman announced, pointing his Uzi at some air bubbles that rode along the surface near a cluster of river ferns.

The other thug promptly opened fire on the plants. Bullets ripped apart leaves and sent sprays of water jetting into the sky. A cry of agony rose from the rattling report of the Uzi. The gunman ceased fire and both men waded toward the brush. They raised their weapons overhead as the waterline reached chest level.

"*Cristo,*" one of them growled as he felt something slither along his leg. Several species of snakes favor the waters of Bolivia . . . including some that are very poisonous.

The *coquito* lieutenant watched from the riverbank, clutching the leather pouch of bank notes attached to his belt by a steel chain. The other two bodyguards stayed with the lieutenant and watched the trio of coca-leaf suppliers, distrustful of the *peones*. The peasants who picked coca leaves for the illegal drug traffic were at the bottom of the barrel in the coke trade, and the hard-nosed *coquitos* did not trust them any more than they trusted anyone else—which is to say, not at all.

"Did you kill them all?" the lieutenant called out to his men in the river.

"We haven't found the third *indio*'s body yet," one of the killers replied. "But I think we got him . . ."

The Indian suddenly lunged from the ferns. Blood oozed from a bullet wound high in his chest, but the man still attacked his tormentors with a machete raised overhead in a two-hand grip. The gunmen were taken off guard by the Indian's sudden aggression. They tried to bring their subguns to bear, but the desperate *indio* was too quick.

The heavy jungle knife struck the closest man in the chest. The sharp blade cleaved through sternal bone and bit deep into the chest cavity. The gunman howled in agony as blood squirted from a terrible wound. The Indian yanked the machete from the dying thug's chest and attacked his second opponent.

The gunman hastily fired his Uzi, cutting a trio of bullet holes in the torso of the charging Indian. Although his body jerked in violent spasms from the 9-mm projectiles, which tore through him like hot rivets through tissue paper, the Indian delivered a final wild swing at his assassin.

The machete struck the triggerman in the side of the head. Sharp steel split skull bone at the left temple. The gunman dropped his Uzi in the water and staggered backward, the machete lodged in the side of his skull, blood and brains oozing down his cheek. He was dead before his body splashed into the river.

"*Madre de Dios,*" the lieutenant muttered, shaking his head as he watched the bodies of his men float beside the corpse of the Indian. "Who would have thought a stinking peasant with a machete could kill two men armed with machine guns."

"He was very brave," a bodyguard remarked, impressed by the Indian's fighting spirit.

The lieutenant turned and swatted the back of his hand across the gunman's face. The bodyguard's head shifted from the blow, but he did not retaliate. Retaliation would not be wise.

"Let's go," the gangster declared with a sigh.

The cold, dry wind blew mercilessly, unimpeded by the sparse vegetation across the altiplano, the intermountain plateau that lies between the eastern and western ranges of the Andes. The old man and the youth reined their horses and gazed over the harsh but beautiful landscape.

The old man had seen the mountains many times before. He was not certain how old he was, since counting years seemed a waste of time to him. The mountains and sky were older than any man. These things were beyond the passing of days and seasons. How important could the age of a single man be? Besides, adding up one's years can be a bit depressing and there are enough negative matters in life without encouraging more.

His bronze leather skin and bottomless mahogany eyes were set off by a long, narrow beaked nose and angular face. He was a pureblood Collahuaya Indian, a branch of the Aymara people, undiluted by the invading Spanish conquistadores or the laborers forcibly imported from Africa to work the silver mines in Potosí.

Spring was approaching. He could do without the heaviest of his winter clothing. No need to wear riding boots. He had switched to his leather sandals, the soles ending just before his toes to give his feet a better grip on the mountain slopes. He wore short pants that ended below his knees and tied at the waist.

The old man ran his fingers over the silver filigree inlaid into the leather of his saddle. He turned and looked at the young man who had patiently and obediently run so many miles beside him to reach this point.

"Now that you have met the norteamericano you must cultivate him and encourage him to use his contacts and the vast resources of his country to find a solution to the problems that plague our people, Raul," the old man instructed.

"I don't know about this one," Raul Metza replied. "The yanqui seems too weak for our purposes. He may never get over altitude sickness long enough to help us."

"You must be patient and give him a chance," the old man counseled. "I have seen the people of his country work before. The norteamericano may be what we need to resolve the threat to our people, but we must also be careful not to place all our hopes in him. If he cannot help us throw off the yoke of El Dorado, we will have to find another way."

"I understand," Raul said with a solemn nod.

"I plan to return from Cuzco in a month," the old man stated. "Unless the situation takes a new turn, you can wait until then to report to me the progress of the norteamericano *federal*. But, if it looks very bad, I will leave word in Cuzco where I can be found."

Raul nodded in reply.

With that, the old man rode on ahead toward Tiquina to catch the ferry across Lake Titicaca. Raul continued on to La Paz on foot, leading his horse by its reins.

Although Sucre is the constitutional capital of Bolivia, La Paz is the seat of the country's government. Raul

Metza had arrived in La Paz and was nervously waiting on the corner of Bueno Street. The Río Choqueyapu extended from Roosevelt Central Park and disappeared into its underground course. Bueno Street is only a block and a half from the broad tree-lined Avenida 16 de julio—more commonly known as El Prado, "the main strip." On Sunday mornings, the young Spanish girls are given to parading on foot in a contemporary version of the promenade while appreciative young men ride countercurrent in a slow procession of motor vehicles.

Night was approaching and, it being the rainy season, Raul was feeling a chill, even through his homespun wool trousers, sweater, and poncho. He untied the earflaps of his skullcap and let them fall to the side of his face.

Raul was anxious to meet with Carlos Rodriguez, the norteamericano *federal* of the United States Drug Enforcement Administration. Rodriguez had previously recruited Raul as a gatherer of field intelligence. The DEA agent had expressed little interest in the European aspects of Bolivian life, but he had asked many questions about the Aymara Indians' comunidad, a word that meant something more than rural settlement or village.

The ayllu, or family grouping was a sacred concept to the Aymara Indians. These values had been conditioned into Raul by the elders of the village from the time he was a young boy. These ideas included territoriality, justice, and distrust of outsiders. Only because the norteamericano *federal* had referred directly to the village's current problem had Raul replied to him at all and only then with the permission of those in authority within the village.

At last, Carlos Rodriguez approached. His rented car labored fitfully up the hill toward Raul. The gasoline engine was designed for the richer air of the coastal areas. It was no surprise to the driver that the car's performance suffered. La Paz is situated in a canyon at an altitude of 11,900 feet in the Andean altiplano.

Rodriguez pulled to the curb and stopped. He opened the door and looked out at Raul. The youth gathered his woolen poncho tightly around his flanks with one hand and ducked his head as he got into the car.

"Cold night to be out on the street," Rodriguez remarked.

"We must go northeast," Raul told the agent. "Over the Cordillera Real and down into the villages of the Yungas where my people live. What I have to show you is there."

"I sure hope so," Rodriguez commented. "Be nice if something went right during this assignment."

The American DEA agent had been sent to Bolivia when the government officials there had indicated their willingness to permit the United States to help them combat the growing illegal cocaine traffic. Since the majority of Bolivian-grown coke is exported to America, the U.S. had a greater reason to cut off the supply than the Bolivians themselves.

The criminal organization responsible for the drug commerce in Bolivia was known as El Dorado, sometimes called the "Cocaine Mafia" or the "Bolivian Mafia." El Dorado was a powerful, wealthy, and extremely ruthless organization, which sometimes joined forces with similar "cocaine families" in Columbia. However, the Colombian government had cracked down on the *coquitos* following the murder of Justice Minister Rodrigo Lara Bonilla in 1985. El Dorado had not been subjected to any serious setbacks, so the Bolivian coke gangsters were rapidly taking the lead in the drug trade.

Rodriguez, like most DEA personnel chosen for assignments in South America, was a Hispanic who was conversant in some form of the Spanish language—usually the "Tex-Mex" dialect spoken in Texas. His superiors had failed to take into account that only about half the citizens of Bolivia even spoke Spanish, and most of these in the urban areas far from where the illicit cocaine was grown and processed.

When Rodriguez first arrived in Bolivia, he thought he still had a chance of carrying off his cover and completing his assignment. His education had not prepared him for the world of difference between the United States and Bolivia. Bolivia's justice system is an odd one, composed of British and Napoleonic traditions. The British influence was codified and inherited from the Roman Empire while the traditions of Napoleon were based largely on one's personal affiliation.

The U.S. State Department figured if a man looked Hispanic, spoke Spanish, and had the ostensible permission of the host country to carry out activities in Latin America, he couldn't go wrong. They failed to appreciate the "Good Ol' Boy" network in Bolivia, where bribes, bluster, and who-you-know have more influence on the justice system than official laws and criminal prosecution procedures according to the book.

"Damn," Rodriguez growled as he felt a blood vessel rupture in his nose.

He rummaged quickly in his coat pocket for a tissue. *I hope that's the only blood that gets spilled before I leave this miserable country,* the DEA agent thought. Rodriguez sought to stanch the flow of blood from his nostril and grabbed for an aspirin and a can of cola in a plastic tray under the dashboard. It was the only medication available to him that seemed to help the incessant headaches that plagued Rodriguez since he arrived at the altiplano of Bolivia. The physician at the U.S. embassy had told him he had classical symptoms of altitude sickness and warned him of other signs, including nosebleeds and spots before his eyes. The predictions had been right on.

So far the DEA agent's stay in Bolivia had fatigued him with the altitude illness and frustrated him due to his inability to penetrate the power structure of the cocaine trade. What the DEA needed, Rodriguez concluded, were more agents like his associate Victor Garcia, who had been born in Bolivia and later became a naturalized U.S. citizen.

Garcia had grown up on the high plateau, and he was accustomed to the altitude and the variety of people that make up the population of Bolivia. Rodriguez felt like shit from the altitude and he still had trouble telling an *indio* from a cholo, or a campesino from a mestizo. He might look like what the DEA thought a "Hispanic" should look like, but Rodriguez could conduct field interviews in his Tex-Mex Spanish every day for a year and still stand out like a blood stain on white linen.

"Are we leaving or not?" Raul Metza asked in a puzzled tone. He couldn't understand why the yanquis had so much trouble with the altitude, and concluded the norteamericanos were even stranger than the Europeans.

"We're going," Rodriguez assured him, dabbing blood from his nose as he washed down two aspirin with lukewarm cola.

The car headed up the mountain road toward Chuspipata. Raul turned and gazed back at the city of La Paz. The lights of the streets and buildings sparkled invitingly from twelve thousand feet. Raul thought La Paz was more attractive from a distance than close up.

Raul directed Rodriguez toward the east, deeper into the Cordillera Real—into areas where the road was little more than a scratch in the side of the upward-thrusting, verdant, scrub-covered walls of granite. Rodriguez felt his heart booming in his chest, trying unsuccessfully to deliver an adequate amount of oxygen to the cells of his body.

They crested the final pass and began the downward descent. Clouds seemed to merge into the earth, forming a low-lying fog. The landscape appeared surreal as clouds billowed down the side of the mountain and rendered everything hazy and indistinct.

The two men were presently in the Yungas, a region made up of sharply tilted mountain valleys that descended

to the east from the peaks of the Cordillera Real. From
three thousand to nine thousand feet in altitude, the region
was semitropical, consisting of narrow river valleys with
heavy precipitation, fertile soils, and constant bountiful
harvests of whatever one wished to grow. It was the most
fertile part of Bolivia, but the steep slopes and eroded
gorges made roads of any kind difficult to establish and
maintain.

Metza directed Rodriguez onto a narrow turnout off the
descending mountain road.

"We are near the village," Raul said, indicating a small
settlement of white adobe dwellings strewn individually
across the steep mountainside.

"Your village?" Rodriguez asked, able to breathe a bit
easier as the altitude tapered off.

"No," Raul replied, "but my village is close and the
two comunidades are very similar. Drive slowly. I will
show you a road that starts beyond the next bend. It leads
to some undergrowth where we can hide this car."

"Why do we have to hide my car?" the DEA agent
asked.

"It'll be safer that way," Raul answered.

They concealed the vehicle and traveled to the village
on foot. Carlos Rodriguez raised his shirt to the small of
his back and drew a .380-caliber Astra Constable from a
pancake holster inside his belt. The weapon appeared to be
in functional condition and the safety catch was on with a
cartridge in the spout. He didn't think he'd need the pistol,
but it was still comforting to know he had it—just in case.

They walked to the village. The adobe structures were
crude, but functional. Flames flickered from small campfires and goats bleated as the strangers approached. The
Aymara villagers watched the pair with distrust and cowered back toward their dwellings. Raul Metza called out to
them in the Aymara tongue.

One of the elder members of the comunidad stepped

forward and spoke with Raul. Callos Rodriguez stood by, unable to understand a word uttered by the Indians. Raul finally turned to the DEA agent.

"This man is Emmanuel Ortega," Raul explained. "He's the jefe, the chief of the village. Señor Ortega said you'll be given clothing that suits the village. He asks that you change clothes so you will appear to be one of us, although he asks that you also remain out of sight during your stay here. This is for your sake as well as ours."

"What are you people scared of?" Rodriguez asked. "Aren't all these precautions a little silly?"

"You'll understand more after we speak with the elders," Raul assured him.

The DEA agent felt awkward as he sat on the dirt floor of Ortega's dwelling and listened to Raul's translations of the jefe's complaints.

"First the government tells us we must sell all of our coca-leaf crop to them at their prices," the elder stated. "Then they tell us they will buy no more this season and that we will not be allowed to sell to anyone else! The coca baled and stored from this year's harvest molders in the shed. My family has lost seventy thousand pesos this year."

"Tell him I'm sorry," Rodriguez sighed. "But I'm not even part of the Bolivian government. There's nothing I can do about it."

Raul didn't get a chance to translate the American's remarks as Ortega continued to talk, forcing Raul to rapidly translate more Aymara into English.

"A man came to us and claimed to be a friend of a high official in the government," Ortega declared. "He offered to buy our unsold crop. His offer was ridiculously low. When we told him that such a transaction would be illegal and refused to deal with him, he warned us that our village would suffer for this decision. Soon afterward, they came and took several hostages—"

"Wait a minute," Rodriguez said sharply. "*Who* came? What's he talking about?"

"Men with guns," Raul explained. "You might call them bandidos or brigands. They took villagers hostage. Relatives of farmers, but not people directly involved in the growing and harvesting of the coca crop. They told the village that the hostages would be safe if the farmers kept up their quotas. It was a very bad thing."

"Didn't they report this to the authorities?" Carlos asked.

"The secretary-general of the province," Ortega explained through Raul's translations, "our regional governor, will do nothing. He is in the pay of the Weisals, our former patrons before the revolution. The Weisal land holdings were split up and distributed among the local campesinos, but the Weisals became successful merchants by deceit and coercion. They are now the local warlords."

"Weisals?" Rodriguez frowned. "Doesn't sound like a Spanish name. Hell, Raul, what do they want me to do about this? I can't get their money back for the lost coca leaves. I was sent here to try to stop the coke trade. I'm gonna tell my superiors what Señor Ortega said about the Weisals—whoever they are—but I doubt that the DEA can do anything about it unless we can convince the Bolivian central government to authorize action. Frankly, I'm not sure that's gonna happen. From what I've seen of the government officials so far, they can be bought off by anybody with enough cash and influence. The Weisals sound like they probably have both."

"Then there is nothing you can do?" Raul frowned.

"Well," the DEA agent began, "we might be able to get the embassy to pressure the government to take action—*if* we can get enough evidence to convince Washington that these guys are big shots in El Dorado. Meantime, there's an outside chance that my government might be willing to provide this village with economic assistance for shifting to another cash crop."

"We don't want your government's money," Ortega retorted, offended by the suggestion. "Before the revolution in 1952, my people lived by barter. It was a poor but honorable existence. What we want is to rid ourselves of these gangsters and have our loved ones returned safely."

"You might want too much," Rodriguez said grimly.

The unexpected thunder of engines interrupted the meeting. The noise of a poorly patched muffler barked above the rumbling of the other machines. The unrestrained detonations from within its cylinder heads reverberated against the dense scrub undergrowth clinging to the slopes that surrounded the village on all sides.

Excited and alarmed voices within the village buzzed outside the chief's adobe house. Ortega spoke to Raul in tense Aymara.

"They're here," Raul told the DEA agent. "It will be very bad for all of us if they find you here."

"You mean the brigands?" Rodriguez asked, eyes wide with astonishment. "They're here *now*?"

"Yes," Raul answered. "Hurry. You must hide in the bushes and stay out of sight."

Rodriguez scrambled from the dwelling. Several vehicles had parked near the village, headlights pointed at the comunidad. The glare of white light illuminated the village, but Rodriguez had emerged on the blind side and managed to scurry to the cover of the bushes where he hoped he'd be unseen by the night raiders.

From his hiding place, the DEA agent watched as several figures approached. They were dressed in American-made Levi's and khaki shirts. Their headgear varied from baseball caps to the British-style felt bowler popular with the Bolivians. All were armed with automatic weapons and most carried side arms on their hips as well. Rodriguez held his breath as gimbal-mounted flood lamps swiveled back and forth from two of the larger vehicles.

One gunman prodded an older Indian male forward with

the barrel of an Uzi submachine gun. The weapon's top-mounted charging lever and distinctive front sight were easily discernible in the harsh illumination of the flood lamps. Carlos Rodriguez felt his spine tingle with fear. Christ, when Raul mentioned bandidos, the DEA agent had pictured dirty halfwits with sombreros and ammo belts crisscrossing their bloated torsos. He had expected to see refugees from *The Treasure of Sierra Madre,* armed with rusty six-guns and old Winchesters, not steely-eyed killers packing modern weapons with fearsome firepower. His Astra pistol seemed as worthless as a rabbit's foot against such odds.

A tall man stepped from the vehicles and strode forward with the casual arrogance of a man accustomed to command. Athletically trim with broad shoulders and a thick chest, the man wore matching tan shirt and trousers like a uniform. His polished jackboots stamped the ground as he marched forward, and a gun belt around his waist contained a pistol in a canvas button-flap holster. A long dagger hung from a short chain attached to his belt, the blade sheathed in a brass scabbard. A silver skull decorated the butt of the knife hilt.

Rodriguez guessed the tall man to be the leader. He glimpsed rakishly handsome features beneath the bent bill of the man's tan cap. The face was lean with a lantern jaw, firm mouth, and narrow nose. His cobalt blue eyes peered icily at the frightened villagers as he approached them.

The DEA agent leaned forward to get a better look. A shape suddenly appeared beside him. Rodriguez realized he'd screwed up and tried to raise his hands to protect himself. But he was too slow. Something hard struck him across the back of the skull. The DEA fell flat on his belly, his nose striking the earth. Pain lanced through his head and warm liquid gushed from his nostrils.

"*¡Señor Weisal, mira aquí!*" the man who had slugged

Rodriguez called out as he stood over the momentarily dazed American.

Rodriguez was hauled roughly to his feet by two bandits and rudely escorted to where the villagers had been rounded up. They shoved him in with the other captives.

"The *indio* wants to get a better look at us," a captor declared in Spanish. "Hey, campesino, you know the rules when we are here."

"Should we leave him with the others or make an example of him, jefe?" another bandit asked the tall man with the Nordic features.

Rodriguez noticed Raul Metza in the middle of the huddled group of Aymaras. The youth's eyes bugged out with fear and anticipation. The DEA agent lowered his head and began a sly, furtive shuffle sideways to try to lose himself in the crowd.

"Un momento!" the bandit chief snapped, deciding to have a better look at the captive.

Rodriguez realized his number was about up. He was ringed by at least ten opponents armed with submachine guns. Carlos figured if he could get outside the ring of illumination formed by the spotlights, he might stand a chance. As one of the bandits stepped forward, Rodriguez made his move. He violently body-checked the brigand with a hip and sent the man hurtling into one of his comrades. Both men collapsed as Rodriguez reached under his poncho and pulled his Astra .380 pistol. He snapshot two rounds at the group of armed men to urge them to keep their heads down.

A bandit in front of the leader groaned and doubled up with a bullet in his belly. Rodriguez quickly fired two more rounds into the pair of bandits he had knocked to the ground. A ragged bullet hole appeared between the shoulder blades of one opponent. Another .380 round burrowed into the throat of the second gunman. The bandit wheezed as he clutched his throat and crumpled to the ground.

Rodriguez ran downhill as the raiders manning the search-lights rotated them on their gimbals, searching out his location. The DEA agent approached an elevated outcrop-ping of undergrowth. It loomed in front of the desperate American like a promise of salvation, almost within reach.

A trio of .45-caliber slugs from a stuttering MAC-10 machine pistol lifted him off his feet. The bullets shattered his backbone and Rodriguez's broken body fell to the ground, limbs splayed outward.

The triggerman with the MAC-10 rushed forward, fol-lowed by two of his comrades, oblivious to the huddled villagers behind them. They dashed to the dead agent's still form, ripping away the campesino poncho and kicking a borrowed bowler derby from his head.

"I think this one was a norteamericano," the gun-sel with the Ingram chatterbox announced with a smile. "Yanqui *federal*. *¿Sí?* There is a bounty offered for these gringo pigs. Is that not so, Señor Weisal?"

"You'll get a reward," the bandit chief assured him. "You did your job well, amigo."

A companion of the killer helped haul the corpse by its heels up the incline. In the confusion no one noticed that Raul Metza had quietly slipped away from the villagers, and was now making his way deep into the underbrush.

CHAPTER 2

"IT'S ABOUT TIME we got my orderly room back in order," John McShayne said gruffly as he sat at the keyboard to a newly installed computer.

"Pretty bad when you have a disorderly orderly room," Joe Fanelli commented with a wiry grin. "Huh, Top?"

"If I want any shit from you, I'll squeeze your head," McShayne growled, fingers dancing across the control panel. Numbers and data appeared on the green viewscreen.

McShayne grunted with satisfaction as he examined the information. The new computer was the same make and model as the machine he had previously used before it was destroyed during a battle within the compound. Most of the diskettes had survived the attack, thanks to the special vault that protected the computer files from damage.

"How's the new machine, Top?" William O'Neal inquired as he entered the orderly room.

"It'll work just fine, Captain," McShayne answered. "Unlike some things around here."

The "top" sergeant stared at Fanelli.

"Hell, Top," the tough Italian from Jersey complained, "I've been workin' my ass off for the last two months."

"We've all been doing that, Joe," O'Neal replied. "Rebuilding this place hasn't been easy, but it had to be done and now we've finally got it finished.''

O'Neal didn't feel like listening to any of his men bitch. The Hard Corps commander had participated in rebuilding the billets, storage houses, head shed and the rest. O'Neal had been born and raised in a Chicago slum. At seventeen, he had enlisted in the U.S. Army and become a member of Special Forces assigned to duty in Vietnam. His potential for leadership led to officer candidate school and he eventually found himself in charge of a special elite team that came to be known as the Hard Corps.

None of this training and experience had prepared O'Neal for amateur carpentry or installing electrical wiring. He was a warrior, accustomed to commanding other warriors in combat. Handyman work wasn't his line and he didn't like being in situations where he felt ignorant and out of his element. McShayne got along well with machines. So did Fanelli to a lesser degree. O'Neal only cared about the ends to which such contraptions could be put.

The last two months had been frustrating for O'Neal. He'd spent them shoving wires through holes in walls, driving nails where others told him they belonged, and following instructions from people who knew more about these things than he did. He hoped they'd soon find another war to fight.

The Hard Corps had been born on the battlefields of Southeast Asia during the Vietnam Conflict—as the history books like to call it. O'Neal's team did their job better than anyone else. Their job wasn't complicated, but it wasn't easy either. They occasionally trained South Vietnamese troops and organized villages for combat. Sometimes they gathered intelligence for SOG. But their primary job was simply to kill the enemy, and they were very good at it.

After American involvement in Vietnam ended in 1975,

O'Neal was unable to readjust to civilian life. This was partly due to popular public opinion at the time, which regarded Vietnam veterans with distrust and distaste if not outright disgust; and partly because O'Neal was different. He had found his role in life on the battlefield and he didn't seem to fit in anywhere else. So O'Neal found a new kind of war.

William O'Neal and three of his former comrades-at-arms resurrected the Hard Corps and became mercenary soldiers of fortune. The term "fortune" had always been a bit misleading, however. The big jobs were few and far between, though eventually the Hard Corps started to earn big money for their biggest missions. Big money usually meant big risks, but that was their specialty anyway.

Their last mission had been the most profitable they'd taken on thus far. It had been a tough assignment in Beirut, rescuing some hostages from a gang of terrorist fanatics. The Hard Corps had received three million dollars for their work.

They needed the money. Shortly before the Beirut contract, the Hard Corps had been attacked on their own turf. More than a hundred killers sent by the Communist government of Vietnam had managed to track a leader of the Southeast Asian resistance fighters to the Hard Corps' compound, here in the state of Washington.

This compound, here in the dense forests of the Northwest, maintained a low profile in order that the Hard Corps operate successfully in their semiclandestine and often not-quite-legal profession. This situation gave them plenty of privacy, but it also left them entirely on their own against the invaders.

The Hard Corps had survived the assault, but the compound had sustained considerable damage. Valuable equipment had been smashed, buildings destroyed, supplies ruined. Repairs and replacements required time and money: the Beirut mission supplied them with the latter. Since the last two months had failed to provide the mercs with any assignments, much to O'Neal's disappointment, they had had the time to finish reconstruction.

At last the task was over. The head shed was back in order, and the hydroelectric and solar-cell power supplies had been replaced. The personal quarters had been rebuilt and furnished. The compound was finally at peak efficiency once again.

"All the computer link-ups with outside sources seem to be restored, sir," McShayne told O'Neal as he continued to test the new computer. "Want me to run some checks to see about prospects for new assignments?"

McShayne was the only member of the team who hadn't been with the Hard Corps in Vietnam, but he was a veteran soldier who'd paid his dues with thirty years' active duty in the United States Army. McShayne had seen combat in Korea and received a Purple Heart in Vietnam. He had been a motor pool mechanic, a supply sergeant, a helicopter mechanic, a mess sergeant, a computer programmer, and a sergeant major. After spending almost two-thirds of his life in uniform, McShayne didn't know how to be a civilian, and he didn't care to learn.

So McShayne had searched for a different kind of army to join. He found a mercenary outfit that was recruiting guys for a mission in Central America.

The Hard Corps had been lucky to get him. McShayne was twenty years older than O'Neal and the retired army vet realized he couldn't charge around in the jungles with the younger troops. He was still a very fit and healthy man, stocky and muscular and more active than many men half his age. McShayne wasn't a combat soldier, but his role was just as vital.

The "top" sergeant ran most of the outfit's functions behind the lines. He handled bookkeeping, communications, supplies, and gathering most of the intelligence information for the unit. McShayne was also the mess sergeant and chief mechanic at the compound.

"Hell," O'Neal told the first sergeant, "we're not hurting for money right now thanks to that last mission. After busting our butts for two months, I figure we can all use a little R and R before we get back to work."

"Now you're talkin', Captain," Fanelli agreed cheerfully. "We gonna head into Seattle and party hardy for a couple days?"

"Just be careful how you party, Joe," O'Neal warned.

"Come on, Captain," Fanelli groaned. "I haven't had a drink for years . . ."

"No," the Hard Corps commander confirmed. "You kept away from the bottle, but you still tend to get in trouble when you go to town. You fuck around like a horny teenager and get in stupid fights as if you left your brain in your quarters before you left the compound."

"I don't get in that many fights," Fanelli insisted. "And I never got any of them social diseases from the girls I slept with. Not even one little dose of clap."

"That either means you've been lucky or you're a little more careful than I gave you credit for being," O'Neal answered.

Fanelli was the youngest member of the Hard Corps mercs, but at thirty-four, he should have grown out of the banty-rooster phase. He'd been a wild kid while growing up in the tough slums of New Jersey, where he liked to participate in drag racing and demolition derbies. Fanelli was already an accomplished street fighter and knife artist even before he joined the army.

He'd always had trouble with authority figures and once nearly got court-martialed before he completed basic training, but Fanelli had learned to keep his mouth shut and put a lid on his short temper. He had a crazy notion about proving himself on the battlefield. Less than five-and-a-half feet tall, Fanelli suffered from an inferiority complex and tried to compensate for it with sheer moxie. His fear of being considered a scrawny runt was grossly exaggerated, but there was no doubt that the guy had balls of solid brass.

Fanelli graduated jump school and went on to become a Green Beret. He wound up in Vietnam with the Hard Corps. The tough kid from Jersey got his chance to prove himself—over and over again. He'd become an expert in demolitions and explosives as well as small arms and hand-to-hand combat. More important, the social misfit finally fit in as a member of an elite fighting unit.

He earned medals for valor, although every time he got a leave in Saigon he seemed to get in trouble for dealing black-market booze and cigarettes, or running a whorehouse—where he tended to be his own best customer. The gutsy soldier finally caught a couple of bullets and wound up stateside in a VA hospital for the last months of his military career.

When he got out and returned home, there wasn't any hero's welcome waiting for him in the streets of New Jersey. He found he was even a bigger misfit than before and started hitting the bottle hard and heavy. His drinking cost him a job, got him arrested, and eventually led to a detox ward at another VA hospital.

Joe Fanelli might have wound up on skid row with cheap wine on his breath and vomit stains on his clothes. That was the path he was headed for when William O'Neal and James Wentworth found him. Fanelli got his shit together so he could join the revived Hard Corps. He stayed away from the booze and he generally kept the hell-raising to a minimum. Still, a lot of that wild street-kid mentality was still a part of Fanelli's personality.

"I'll behave," Fanelli promised. He shrugged as he added, "More or less."

"You're not going to Seattle alone," O'Neal told him. "None of us are and we're not going all together . . .

Hell, I might as well tell everybody and save having to repeat myself like a goddamn parrot.''

The team leader and Fanelli left the head shed. McShayne was still busy with his computer and radios. "Top" didn't need to hear O'Neal's lecture. He'd already guessed what the captain had in mind and it was okay with him.

O'Neal and Fanelli found James Wentworth III outside his cottage. Wentworth was clad in a white cotton gi uniform with a black belt knotted around his rather paunchy waist. He held a wood sword in his fists as he practiced a series of kata.

Wentworth moved smoothly and gracefully in the combat exercise forms, slashing the *bokken* practice sword in unison with his footwork. He often said that breath control and footwork were as important in *kenjutsu* as the sword strokes delivered. Wentworth also claimed he found inner peace through Japanese fencing. Maybe so, but the other members of the Hard Corps were more impressed by the permanent "peace" Wentworth had given to several enemies with a sword in the past.

James Wentworth III was an oddball—a fairly common character trait among elite fighting men. Yet Wentworth, unlike O'Neal and Fanelli, wasn't a product of a big-city slum. He had been born to a fairly wealthy oil family in Oklahoma. James III had been reared on horseback riding, hunting on the weekends, and a little trapshooting from time to time. He had gone to expensive private schools and later to West Point.

West Point had been a Wentworth tradition since 1802—the year it became a military academy. Wentworth men had fought in every American war since the Revolution. James III naturally followed in this tradition. He graduated West Point with honors and became an officer in the Green Berets.

Eventually, Lieutenant Wentworth was assigned to the Hard Corps team and served as O'Neal's second-in-command. He had continued as the Hard Corps executive officer after the unit became a mercenary outfit.

"Jim," O'Neal began, "you wanna put that thing down for a while? I want everybody together for a talk."

"Appears you've got everybody except Caine," Wentworth remarked. "Good luck trying to find him."

"God damn it," O'Neal snorted. "I'm getting tired of that guy slinking away into the forest to play survival games."

"Steve says he needs time to himself," Fanelli commented. "You know how he is. The guy was always sort of a loner even before he got involved with the Katu—"

"This isn't a retreat for communion with nature," O'Neal said gruffly. "And the Hard Corps has to work as a team and everybody in this outfit had damn well better be a team player."

"I always have been when it counts, sir," a familiar voice declared from behind O'Neal and Fanelli.

The Hard Corps commander involuntarily jerked about, startled by the unexpected presence of the tall, lean man who had padded silently up behind him. O'Neal managed to stifle a gasp of surprise. His face flushed with anger and a degree of embarrassment as he realized Caine had once again crept up on him without being detected.

"One of these days you're gonna pull that stunt and one of us is gonna blow your head off before we realize it's you," O'Neal warned, glaring at Caine.

This was not an idle threat. The mercenaries were always armed. O'Neal always carried a .45-caliber 1911A1 Colt pistol on his hip. Fanelli usually carried a .45 and a .357 snub-nosed revolver for backup. He had formerly used a .38 Special for a hold-out piece, but after he'd literally emptied a snub gun of this caliber into an opponent who still kept coming, Fanelli had switched to a weapon with magnum power instead.

McShayne favored a .44 magnum Smith & Wesson.

"Top" seldom left the compound and he usually didn't participate directly in combat situations. The big wheel gun wasn't the best choice for combat since the hefty recoil made rapid fire almost impossible and the revolver required more time to reload than an autoloading pistol—even with the use of a speed loader. However, McShayne was a bit paranoid about the occasional black bears that roamed about the five-hundred-acre compound. He wanted something powerful enough to stop a big hairy beast dead in its tracks. The .44 mag suited that purpose.

Wentworth generally carried a .45 and frequently had some other sort of weapon as well. The West Point officer liked to carry a swagger stick from time to time. This wasn't just vanity: Wentworth could use the stick for what it had originally been designed for—as a weapon. He also had a katana and *wakazashi,* the long and short swords of the samurai, and he could use either with deadly efficiency.

In addition, all the mercs were also trained in hand-to-hand combat. Knife fighting, clubs, boxing, karate, jujitsu, aikido, and just plain dirty tricks were among their skills. Creeping up behind guys like the Hard Corps could be a fatal mistake.

Of course, Steve Caine realized this. He was as lethal as any of his fellow teammates, and fully understood their aggravation and concern that battle-honed reflexes could lead to tragedy. Caine didn't sneak about silently on purpose. Stealth had been conditioned into him during his years with the Katu. Moving with the silence of a serpent was as natural for Caine as putting one foot in front of the other.

Even as a kid, Steve Caine had been a moody loner. He'd tried to break this syndrome when he married during his senior year of high school, but the young couple was neither emotionally nor financially able to make the union work. After the divorce, Caine drifted for almost a year before a fight with some foul-tempered winos landed him in a courtroom.

The judge gave him an option: go to jail for a year or enlist in the armed forces. Caine chose the latter. He decided that if he had to be in uniform he might as well try for something special, so he signed up to be a Green Beret.

He learned a lot about himself in the Army. Caine discovered he had greater strength and endurance than he'd ever imagined before. He had a knack for linguistics and enrolled in a course in Vietnamese. Caine also learned to work together with others, although he still needed time away from his teammates to allow his mind to find comfort in the sanctuary of solitude.

While with the Special Forces in Vietnam, Caine developed a special kind of rapport with the Montagnards, the primitive mountain people of Southeast Asia. While most Westerners couldn't begin to relate to the Montagnards, Caine felt a strange kinship with these people who were regarded as alien life-forms within their own country.

Of all the Montagnard tribes, the least understood and most widely feared had been the Katu. Fearless hunters and fierce warriors, the Katu had mastered the deadly arts of jungle warfare and specialized in stealth, camouflage, and night fighting. They were feared by the South Vietnamese as well as the NVA and the Vietcong. Even the other Montagnards regarded the Katu as savages who would not hesitate to kill at the slightest provocation and still performed human sacrifices. Indeed, the Katu reputation was founded upon truth.

Yet Caine found a bizarre beauty in the simplicity and savagery of the Katu. He felt their rules weren't that different from any other culture, except the Katu were more direct, more honest. Caine learned the language and customs of the Katu. Eventually, Caine even married a Katu woman in the wedding ritual of her tribe.

Then Caine's second chance for happiness was torn from his grasp. His new bride was killed during an NVA attack, less than a month before the Hard Corps were

scheduled to pull out of Vietnam. When the others prepared to return to the States, Steve Caine slipped away and
joined the Katu. He remained in Vietnam for three years,
fighting the Communist forces as a Katu guerrilla warrior.

When the last of his Katu brothers was killed, Steve
Caine finally left Vietnam. He trekked across Laos to Thai-
land, where he learned of a mercenary team that was
planning to rescue some American POWs from a prison
hidden in the jungles of Laos. Caine met with the mercenaries, hoping to join their unit. To his astonishment, he
discovered the soldiers of fortune were Captain O'Neal,
Lieutenant Wentworth, and Sergeant Fanelli. The Hard
Corps was reunited at last.

"Sorry, sir," Caine now told O'Neal with a shrug. "I
didn't do it on purpose."

"I know, I know," O'Neal said with exasperation.
"Just try to make a little more noise from time to time."

"Maybe we should tie a cowbell around his neck,"
Wentworth suggested, only half joking.

"We got everybody together, Captain," Fanelli reminded
O'Neal, eager to find out when they'd be going on R and
R.

"We got a mission?" Wentworth asked. His tone suggested he wouldn't object to getting into action again.

"No, we don't," O'Neal answered. "And we're not
even gonna look for one just yet. We've been humping our
butts to get the compound fixed up and I'm happy to
announce we're finally finished. Top's hooked up his computer and it's working just fine. That was the last item that
needed to be repaired or replaced. Gentlemen, the job is
officially done."

"Hoorah!" Fanelli exclaimed. "Now let's go get laid."

"Sometimes I think you must have a cock for a brain,
Joe," O'Neal muttered.

"Thanks, Captain," Fanelli replied cheerfully.

"Anyway," O'Neal began, figuring Fanelli was men-

tally locked onto one subject for the moment and unable to
think rationally about anything else, "I feel we've all
earned a little R and R."

"Personally," Wentworth began, "I'd rather be fighting people again than wrestling with nails and boards."

"Don't listen to him, Captain," Fanelli urged. "We
need to get our ashes hauled before we take on any
assignments."

"As a matter of fact," O'Neal replied, "I agree with
you . . . more or less. We all need to get among regular
people for a while. We need to loosen up."

O'Neal realized that R and R wasn't just an excuse to
have fun. Too much work and stress isn't good for combat
troops. They can lose their edge, like a blade that's been
ground down too often. Soldiers can be overconditioned
by too many missions and too much training. Such men
are apt to overreact to the slightest implied threat. Some
overconditioned soldiers aren't even able to mingle safely
with other people on the street.

O'Neal had experienced this himself right after 'Nam. If
a man reached inside his coat, O'Neal tensed up and
prepared to jump the guy in case he drew a gun instead of
a pack of cigarettes. If somebody bumped into him on a
subway he'd have to consciously fight his reflexes before
he lashed out with an elbow smash or a back kick. His mind
told him that it was very unlikely somebody on the Chicago
subway would knife or garrote him, but the conditioned
responses at the stem of his brain sent a different message.

"Okay," O'Neal began. "We'll leave the compound in
pairs. Jim and Steve will leave together . . ."

"I'd like to spend some more time here," Wentworth
commented. "I've got a lot of new books and tapes which
I haven't had a chance to study."

"I'm not in any hurry to leave either," Caine remarked.
"Since we've had to spend most of our time rebuilding the
compound, I haven't been able to live in the forest . . ."

"You can play Tarzan any time," Fanelli complained, afraid his two eccentric teammates were going to ruin the leave for everyone.

"We are *all* taking a vacation from this place and that's an order," O'Neal insisted. "Since you two want to hang around here with books and bushes, Fanelli and I will leave first."

"Now you're talking, Captain," Fanelli said eagerly.

"We'll be gone for one week," O'Neal explained. "When we get back, Jim and Steve will go on leave. I don't care if you don't enjoy yourselves, so long as you associate with other people to some degree. You guys are gonna go stir-crazy if you don't get out of here more often."

"What about Top?" Caine inquired. "He has to spend more time here than any of us."

"McShayne can take his leave now or later," the Hard Corps commander replied. "That's up to him. If he wants to spend a while with filing and bookkeeping, that's his decision, but he's sure as hell earned a holiday and he can leave now if he wants."

"That's mighty generous, sir," McShayne announced as he approached the group. "But I don't think any of us oughta pack our bags just yet."

"What the hell does that mean?" Fanelli asked with a frown.

"I just got a radio message from Old Saintly," McShayne declared. "He called to let us know he's on his way here. The helicopter will be arriving in about twenty minutes."

"Tell him to go fuck himself," Fanelli growled.

"At ease, Joe," O'Neal said. "We'd better find out what he wants."

"God damn it," Fanelli moaned. "I just know that son of a bitch is gonna screw us outta our leave."

CHAPTER 3

JOSHUA ST. LAURENT was a case officer for the Central Intelligence Agency stationed on duty assignment in Canada, where he gathered covert information on embassy personnel from various foreign countries as well as spying on the Canadians themselves. He was also the official liaison officer for the Hard Corps and the federal government.

Although Uncle Sam didn't officially approve of mercenaries, the government occasionally found elite private groups of paramilitary professionals to be useful—especially when the U.S. had a problem that needed to be taken care of without direct involvement by the government.

The CIA learned about the Hard Corps and realized the potential advantages of forming an alliance with the mercenaries. So St. Laurent was ordered to contact the Hard Corps and make a deal with them. The CIA would keep federal heat off the mercs and occasionally pass on information and advice that might help with their missions. In return, the Company would expect the Hard Corps to do them a "favor" or two from time to time.

When St. Laurent climbed out of the helicopter at the Hard Corps 'copter pad, O'Neal was waiting for him. The expression on the mercenary's face wasn't exactly cheer-

ful, but the CIA officer displayed a wide grin. It was the
sort of expression politicians use when they're running for
office. The smile did absolutely nothing to brighten O'Neal's
attitude.

"Hello, Captain," St. Laurent declared as he ducked
his head beneath the whirling rotor blades of the chopper.
"Been a while since we met face-to-face."

"Uh-huh," O'Neal replied dryly. "So what do you
want, Saintly?"

"Why do you people insist on calling me by that ridicu-
lous nickname?" the CIA officer asked with a sour
expression.

"It's not as bad as some of the things we could call
you," O'Neal remarked as he led St. Laurent away from
the helipad. "I don't like repeating myself, Saintly. What
do you want?"

"We've got a mission for you," St. Laurent explained.

"Sorry," O'Neal answered. "This cab is not in service.
You'll have to take somebody else for a ride."

"It's not a request, O'Neal," Saintly told him. "You
fellas owe the Company a favor, especially after I tipped
you off for that Beirut job with Malcolm Banks."

"Oh, yeah," O'Neal said sarcastically. "You guys
did us a big favor. The Company couldn't begin to find
the hostages in Lebanon. CIA didn't even give us any
weapons when we arrived in the Middle East. From
beginning to end, we had to handle the whole show on our
own."

"Thought that's how you guys liked to operate," Saintly
said with a shrug.

"We don't like to rely on anybody else because other
people aren't reliable," the Hard Corps leader answered.
"Or do I have to remind you who it was who sent Trang
Nih to our base without telling us in advance? Christ, that
whole thing ended up like 'Nam all over again."

"So I made a mistake," Saintly admitted. "I still got

you that deal with Banks. We figure he paid you at least two million for that job. I'd say that makes us even."

"Even, sure," O'Neal agreed. "But we don't owe the Company any favors."

"Uncle Sam doesn't look at it that way," the CIA guy stated. "In fact, Uncle could consider your merry band of mercs to be criminals. Tax fraud alone could land you all in a federal prison. Then there's the matter of illegal automatic weapons and explosives that haven't been licensed or approved by the BATF. A number of your missions could also be considered violations of international law. We can even drag up the fact one of your guys, Steve Caine, went AWOL in Vietnam and is still listed as missing in action. Some might call that desertion in a combat situation."

"That wasn't the reason Caine went AWOL and you know it," O'Neal hissed through clenched teeth.

"I know that and you know that," Saintly remarked. "But do you think either one of us would be witnesses at his trial? Tut-tut, O'Neal. Surely you realize if the government wants to fuck you, your ass is grass with a tunnel in the center. The grass will be mowed down to the top soil and the tunnel gets a big, hard shaft with spikes in it."

"And if we don't play ball you'll rape us," O'Neal muttered. "Is that the picture, Saintly?"

"I wouldn't think of such a thing," the CIA agent replied, eyes wide with mock horror. "But it wouldn't be up to me. You understand, don't you?"

"You're just doing your job," O'Neal said dryly. "Just like the Nazi war criminals at Dachau."

"That's not a fair comparison, O'Neal," Saintly replied.

"No," O'Neal admitted. "But you pissed me off with these threats so I figured I'd say something to piss you off in return. Don't push too hard, Saintly. You put the heat on us and we'll take off and set up somewhere else."

"We'd find you," Saintly declared.

"You might be real sorry if you did," O'Neal said with a cold smile. "But let's quit screwing around with this crap, Saintly. Tell me what you want and we'll see if we're gonna butt heads over it."

"We want you to work with the Drug Enforcement Administration in Bolivia," Saintly explained. "You know what they've got in Bolivia?"

"Monkeys, jaguars, and llamas that migrated from Peru," O'Neal answered. "I think it's also the third or fourth largest producer of tin—"

"Cute," Saintly snorted. "I'm talking about cocaine."

"No shit?" O'Neal said with mock surprise. "I thought the U.S. sent troops to Bolivia to help the government fight the coke traffic."

"That's right," St. Laurent confirmed. "And American troops have assisted in several raids on cocaine producers with jungle laboratories."

"So what do you want from us?" O'Neal asked. "The U.S. has already committed troops to combat the cocaine trade. That's no state secret. What more can a handful of mercenaries do?"

"Our military personnel have to play by the rules," Saintly explained. "They're assisting the Bolivian government and they have to pretty much play ball with the officials. Trouble is, a lot of those officials are involved with the dope trade."

"But you said they've raided coke labs," O'Neal remarked.

"Yeah," the CIA officer said with a nod. "But they haven't had any major busts like the Colombians had at Tranquilandia. You remember the incident? It made world news back in '85. They seized fourteen tons of cocaine. The biggest dope bust in history. A month and a half later, the syndicate gunned down the justice minister in the streets of Bogotá."

"I see," O'Neal mused. "The Bolivians are afraid a

major raid might convince the cocaine gangsters to retaliate against government officials the same way."

"Possibly," St. Laurent answered. "Or maybe corrupt officials connected with El Dorado are still protecting the big shots in the outfit."

"El Dorado?" O'Neal raised an eyebrow. "That's the Bolivian version of the Mafia or something like that."

"The Mafia has a nicer bunch of people in it," the CIA officer remarked. "El Dorado is very powerful, very wealthy. The coke trade rakes in about three hundred *billion* dollars a year. Any bunch of gangsters who make that kind of bread can afford to buy off officials, bribe the judges and the police, and purchase state-of-the-art weapons and transportation. They can also have people killed. El Dorado has a bounty on American DEA agents. A hitman can get thirty thousand dollars for wasting a single DEA agent."

"Thirty grand?" O'Neal whistled. "I recall stories about hitmen who were supposedly offered money to assassinate President Kennedy. None of them were offered more than twenty-five thou. Of course, that was back in '63. Cost of killing has probably gone up by now."

"The cost of living goes up and so does the cost of dying," Saintly remarked with a slight smile. "Have you guessed now what your assignment will be?"

"You want us to stop a hundred-billion-dollar illegal business that the DEA, the State Department, and about thirty-five other federal agencies and the combined efforts of half a dozen other governments haven't been able to put a dent in." O'Neal shook his head. "Get real, Saintly. The Hard Corps doesn't perform miracles."

"Nobody expects a miracle," the CIA officer assured him. "But El Dorado has been murdering DEA agents in Bolivia. So far, they've been getting away with it. We want those bastards to know that if they kill our people, we'll hit back. Hard and fast. And we won't be worried about whether it's legal or not.''

"So you want us to be your hit team?'' O'Neal frowned. "We're not murderers, Saintly.''

"You don't have to kill anyone,'' Saintly replied, "although you'll probably have to before the mission is over. All you have to do is find a major coke operation and destroy it. If you can do that without killing anyone, that's okay. Just wreck El Dorado's sense of invulnerability. Let them know if they start killing Americans they'll pay for it one way or the other.''

"You said we'd be working with the DEA?'' O'Neal commented. "Are you sure the guys we'll be working with are secure? If their covers are burned, we'll be screwed before we arrive in Bolivia.''

"Don't worry about that,'' the CIA agent assured him. "We'll take care of contacts you'll need in Bolivia. It'll be easier than Beirut. You won't have to worry about getting weapons or other equipment. Including artificial blood.''

"If that's a joke—'' O'Neal began.

"No joke,'' Saintly said. "We're going to supply you guys with a type of synthetic blood developed by the Japanese as a product of the microencapsulation industry. We've got the blood types of all the Hard Corps members, although I'd better cross-check to make sure our information is correct. Can't have you injecting the wrong type of blood into your veins. That would probably be fatal, you know.''

"Is there a reason for this?'' O'Neal demanded, wondering if the stories he'd heard about the Feds testing new drugs on unsuspecting "volunteers'' might have some truth to them.

"Nothing sinister about it, Bill,'' Saintly assured him. "You see, the high altitude of Bolivia presents a special problem for your people. You're gonna have trouble func-

tioning unless we beef up your blood stream with red
blood cells. This is a practice that was pioneered by professional athletes. They'd take a pint of blood every eight
weeks from an athlete who was going to perform at an area
of the world where altitude sickness might be a problem.
The blood was frozen and stored. When the big competi-
tion came up, the stored blood was thawed and centrifuged
to extract red blood cells, which were then reinjected into
the same athlete's veins.''

"You're serious about this?'' O'Neal asked with a frown.

"Absolutely,'' the CIA agent insisted. "The fortified
blood will allow you to perform at peak efficiency despite
the altitude.''

"Okay, we'll use the blood,'' the Hard Corps commander agreed. "Does the DEA have any idea where we
can find a major El Dorado operation suitable for us to hit,
or do we have to do their job as well as the Company's?''

"I understand DEA has a target in mind,'' Saintly said
dryly, choosing to ignore O'Neal's implication that the
CIA was sending the Hard Corps to do its dirty work.
After all, the remark was partly true. "So this ought to be
a pretty straightforward mission. You go in, meet your
contacts, get your weapons and stuff, hit the bastards, and
haul ass. Simple.''

"At least in theory,'' O'Neal muttered. "But things
don't always go the way you plan them when you're
actually in a combat situation.''

"That's your concern, Captain,'' the CIA officer replied. "We've set up the mission, arranged everything we
could for you. The actual execution of the plan is up to
you. You want the mission?''

"Not really,'' O'Neal admitted. "But I don't think it's
worth the price of turning it down. If we refuse we've
either got to fend off the IRS and whoever else you can sic
on us, or sever all contact with the Company and run.
Better if we take the mission.''

· "Glad to hear it." Saintly smiled.

"Speaking of price," O'Neal added. "Are we gonna get paid anything for this?"

"You'll each receive twenty thousand dollars," Saintly answered. "Half in advance and half after completion of the assignment."

"Twenty grand," O'Neal mused. "El Dorado might pay us more than that if we kill some DEA agents for them."

"Not funny." The CIA man glared at O'Neal. "Watch your mouth around the boys from Drug Enforcement. They might take a remark like that seriously. Since some of their people got wasted in Bolivia, they've lost their sense of humor when it comes to stuff like that. In fact, most of them are probably pretty scared by now."

"With good reason," the Hard Corps commander replied, nodding. "Don't worry about how we'll treat the DEA guys in Bolivia. They're soldiers in the trenches. My team understands that. When do you want us to leave?"

"How does three days sound?" St. Laurent asked.

"Pretty shitty," O'Neal replied. "My men haven't had a decent leave for months. We were all planning to take a little vacation and now I've got to tell them it's canceled."

"I'm sure they'll understand," the CIA officer said with a shrug. "Tell them you'll make it up to them later."

"Great," O'Neal sighed. "Got any other bad news for me, or is that it?"

"That's all for now," Saintly assured him as he turned to head back to the helicopter. "But I'll be in touch."

CHAPTER 4

THE SENTRIES STOOD at attention as Erik Weisal approached. The tall blond man with Nordic features examined the guards with critical cobalt-blue eyes. They wore tan uniforms, similar to Weisal's own outfit. He glanced down at one man's jackboots and frowned.

"Don't you believe in polishing your boots, soldier?" Weisal demanded in flawless Spanish. "I realize we're in the jungle, but you don't have to tramp about in the bush. There's no excuse for a sloppy appearance while standing guard at my father's house."

"*Sí*, señor," the sentry replied with a nod. "I shall dress more carefully from now on."

Weisal's complaint seemed absurd, but the sentry realized the steely-eyed German was serious and it wasn't healthy to disregard an order given by Erik Weisal. The man believed in strict and immediate punishment: Weisal had been known to "execute" individuals who failed to obey his commands.

Weisal examined the sentries' weapons and inspected the chambers and barrels to make certain the submachine guns had been recently cleaned and oiled. He grunted with unenthusiastic satisfaction and returned the weapons to the guards. Both men stood at attention in case Weisal had further instructions.

"Very well," the German began in a frosty tone. "Prepare to continue your duty."

"*Sí, jefe*," a sentry replied, hoping this was what Weisal wanted from him.

The blond man shook his head and stepped back. His left hand clawed open the button-flap holster and he swiftly drew a Walther P-38 and pointed it at the pair. The guards awkwardly fumbled with the bolts of their weapons, attempting to chamber rounds before Weisal shot them down. They realized this was hopeless and froze in mid-action. Weisal slowly raised his pistol to aim the muzzle at the sky.

"Now you think to chamber rounds in your weapons, *ja*?" he remarked, returning the Walther to its holster. "If I had been an enemy, you would both be dead now. To stand guard properly, I expect you to be prepared for action and alert to danger. Take your job seriously or I'll have you replaced by others I can trust. And if you have to be replaced, you won't be working for anyone else. *¿Comprende?*"

The sentries nodded. They fully understood what Weisal meant by this threat. The German pushed open the gate and marched past them to his father's house. The grounds were well cared for, he noted with satisfaction. Grass had been trimmed and weeds uprooted. Orchids and other wildflowers grew in the gardens along the outside of the brick-and-timber dwelling.

Weisal knocked on the door. A balding, rotund man opened it. He smiled and stepped aside to allow Weisal to enter.

"*Guten Tag, Erik*," the other man greeted. "Your father is expecting you."

"*Guten Tag, Herr Doktor*," Weisal replied, closing the door. "How is my father today?"

"He's tired," the doctor explained. "The pains in his chest have started again. Try not to excite him."

"I understand, *Herr Doktor,*" Weisal said with a nod.

His father, Adolf Weisal, had suffered a heart attack in 1983 upon hearing that an old friend had been expelled from Bolivia. The friend, Klaus Barbie, had been delivered into the hands of the French government to stand trial for accusations of atrocities committed during World War II. Adolf Weisal had always felt that he and Barbie were safe in Bolivia. After all, Barbie had been a consultant for the national security apparatus and assisted the central government in putting down political unrest. The French had been trying to have Barbie extradited since 1972, and for an entire decade, these efforts had failed.

Then Barbie was turned over to his enemies. Weisal also had enemies with long memories who still sought to bring Nazi war criminals to justice. The shock of discovering that his sense of security was far less realistic than he'd imagined was too much for the old man's heart. Adolf Weisal had nearly died from the heart attack and suffered a serious stroke in 1985, which left him partially paralyzed. The old man's health had not been his only problem. Fear and paranoia had also taken their toll and reduced a once-confident and commanding figure to a nervous, frightened neurotic.

Few individuals would feel any sympathy for Adolf Weisal. During World War II, he was a young officer in the Third Reich, an SS stormtrooper who assisted in rounding up "undesirables" to be sent to concentration camps in Poland. A devout National Socialist and a fanatical racist, Lieutenant Weisal enjoyed his work and firmly believed that the policies of Adolf Hitler were not only right, but righteous as well.

Toward the end of the war, Adolf Weisal was promoted to captain and served as an assistant to Klaus Barbie in France. The infamous "interrogator" tortured and killed hundreds of prisoners, mostly French Jews. Captain Weisal was a very willing and eager accomplice in this brutal venture.

Weisal and Barbie fled to South America after the war. They wandered from country to country before settling in Bolivia. Barbie continued to move about from time to time, but Weisal made a home in Bolivia and raised a family. His son, Erik Klaus Weisal, was born in Bolivia to a woman of German descent. Adolf Weisal proudly declared that his offspring would be pure Aryans and members of the Master Race that, he still believed, would one day rule the world.

Erik Weisal worshiped his father and admired him for his dedication to National Socialism. However, the younger Weisal was a practical man. The chances of building a Fourth Reich on the ashes and broken dreams of the defeated Third were too small to seriously consider. Old Adolf had still clung to his dreams of glory until Barbie was extradited to France. The incident had crushed the senior Weisal's faith, but it confirmed something Erik had suspected for a long time.

If the Weisal family was ever to achieve true power in the future, it would have to be gained through the shadowy forces of the Bolivian underworld. Erik was convinced of this and exerted his energies in that direction even before the incident with Klaus Barbie. In the late 1960s, Erik Weisal became the leader of a press gang that abducted Indian peasants and forced them to work as slave laborers in tin mines run by unscrupulous companies.

By 1972, the potential profits of cocaine led Weisal to alter the nature of his career. He continued to supply Indian slaves for customers, but concentrated on forced labor for the coca harvests. By the time the great cocaine mafias were formed around 1975, Weisal was already involved in the trade. He became the leader of a splinter group of El Dorado. Weisal's *coquitos* helped supply coca leaves to the large dealers. His people were trained in the use of automatic weapons and often served as bodyguards for other *coquitos*. Weisal also continued his slav-

ery operations by forcing Indians to work for El Dorado or
blackmailing them into producing crops for the gangsters
by abducting hostages and threatening to kill them if the
indios failed to obey orders.

Erik Weisal had been very successful. He had wealth
and power and influence that far exceeded anything his
father had accomplished. Erik was a good son and he took
care of Adolf Weisal as the old man approached his twilight years.

The sight of his father in a wheelchair never failed to
sadden Erik Weisal. The old man was paralyzed from the
waist down and his left arm was frozen in a crooked stance
against his chest. Erik's father was emaciated and shriv-
eled. A royal blue dressing gown hung loosely from the
old Nazi's scrawny frame.

"Erik," the senior Weisal said, lips curled upward in a
gesture that vaguely resembled a smile, "it is good to see
you, my son."

"I told you I would be here today, Father," Erik replied. "Have I ever failed to keep my word?"

"Never," the Nazi agreed as his son sat on the edge of
the sofa near the wheelchair. "Does business go well?"

"*Natürlich,*" Erik Weisal assured him. "Very well.
Alberto Juarez and I have made contact with several villages that will be producing more coca for us. We've
arranged conditions to insure that the peasants will remain
productive and loyal. Then we simply visit them in rota-
tion and make collections."

"You have done well in this land, Erik," Adolf Weisal
sighed. "I am very glad for you. I have never truly
considered Bolivia my home. I miss the Fatherland. It is a
pity you have never been to Germany, but then the Germany of my youth no longer exists. The Americans and
the British took part of it and the Russians took the rest.
They ruined Germany forever. They turned all the Ger-

mans into Americans and Russians who still claim to be Germans and speak the German language.''

"Lots of Americans are dying from cocaine," Erik assured his father. "Hoodlums addicted to cocaine are robbing others to buy the drugs. American females are turning to prostitution to support their habit. We're making them suffer, Father. Find some comfort in this.''

"Make them suffer more, Erik," Adolf Weisal urged. "My old comrades cry out for justice. Mengele, Bormann, Himmler. *Der Führer* himself. They all call out from their graves to me at night. I can hear them as I drift between waking and sleep . . .''

"The Americans will suffer," Erik Weisal promised. "Tell your ghosts to rest easy. America is becoming a drug addict.''

CHAPTER 5

THE HARD CORPS arrived at Viru-Viru Airport in Santa Cruz. Joshua St. Larent had supplied the mercenaries with excellent forged passports and visas. The CIA case officer even gave them a cover story to explain why the four Americans had decided to "take a vacation" together in Bolivia.

Like every good lie, the cover used as much of the truth as possible. The Hard Corps were army buddies who'd served together in Vietnam. According to Saintly's cover story, the four guys had made a pact that if they survived the war in Southeast Asia, they'd get together once a year and travel to different locales in the world to see the sights and share some unique experiences as sort of a celebration that they were still alive. This year the four ex-GIs had decided to go to Bolivia to see the Andes Mountains, Lake Titicaca, and other sights that would appeal to tourists.

The cover story wasn't the best that the Hard Corps had used, but it was better than some they'd used in the past. The tourists gimmick would allow them to enter Bolivia without much hassle. However, O'Neal figured the Bolivian cops might keep an eye on them in case the four "tourists" planned to score a dope deal with El Dorado. Every year hundreds of Americans, mostly kids, head for South America with notions of buying a shitload of cocaine to sell on the streets back in the U.S. All they want is that one big deal that'll make enough money to set them up for life. These get-rich-quick schemes, however, usually end up exploding in their faces.

The Hard Corps had come to damage the coke trade, not profit from it, but they'd still have to watch out for the Bolivian authorities. The central government wouldn't be thrilled about a bunch of yanqui mercs running a private mission in their country. If the Hard Corps got in trouble nobody would bail them out—including the U.S. embassy, the State Department, and the CIA.

Of course, the cops weren't the Hard Corps' main concern. First there was that thirty-thousand-dollar price on the head of any American DEA agent stationed in Bolivia. If El Dorado suspected the Hard Corps were more than tourists, the mercs could become targets before they could get close to their objective.

The mercenaries didn't bring any weapons or unusual gear with the camping equipment in their luggage. The customs officers at Viru-Viru barely glanced at their baggage. The inspectors seemed more concerned that the Hard Corps members' vaccinations against cholera and yellow fever were in order than with what they might have hidden in their luggage.

The Hard Corps were surprised and impressed by Viru-Viru Airport. It was as modern as Chicago-O'Hare or Kennedy International and a hell of a lot neater. Of course, Viru-Viru was less than five years old and it wasn't as busy as most airports in major U.S. cities.

The Hard Corps cashed some traveler's checks and received almost a hundred thousand pesos (less than two thousand dollars). The mercenaries had a slight language barrier to deal with since only O'Neal and Fanelli spoke more than a hundred words in Spanish and neither man was fluent in the language. However, the cashier had handled traveler's checks before so he didn't have much trouble understanding what they wanted.

The mercs purchased plane tickets for a flight to La Paz. They didn't have to wait long because numerous planes take off from Viru-Viru to La Paz every day. The Hard Corps boarded their flight and soon they were headed for the largest city in Bolivia. The view from the air of the city, the highest large city in altitude in the world, was remarkably clear since La Paz has limited industry due to difficulty in maintaining power sources. The lack of smog and factory smoke left the sky crystal clear. Modern buildings towered above the paved streets below. Cars and trucks crept through the city.

After landing at La Paz Airport the Hard Corps took a cab to the La Paz-Sheraton. Nineteen stories tall with 360 rooms, the Sheraton is the largest first-class hotel in La Paz and the most popular with American tourists. No wonder at fifty bucks a night for top-notch accommodations that include free underground parking, an indoor swimming pool, and even a Turkish bathhouse.

The mercenaries checked into their rooms and left their luggage and camping gear in their quarters. Steve Caine took one item from his equipment—a survival knife with a six-inch steel blade. The black handle was hollow and contained emergency survival gear—fishhooks, line and sinkers, matches, and a wire saw that could serve as a garrote. The blade was razor sharp with a sawtooth back, and the black leather sheath included a sharpening stone.

Caine smiled as he tucked the big sheath knife under his belt at the small of his back and covered it with his jacket. The tall bearded mercenary was an expert in primitive survival and he felt naked without his most trusted weapon-tool. Caine joined the other three Hard Corps mercs in the corridor and the four men headed for the stairs.

"Wonderful view of the Andes from our room," Went-worth remarked. He and O'Neal were sharing a double room. "You know, this city is surrounded by mountains."

"Big deal," Fanelli muttered. "So's the compound. I wonder if we can get laid while we're at this dump."

"The Sheraton certainly isn't a dump," Wentworth told him. "But what would you know about quality hotels? Your tastes lean toward fleabags where they have to change the bed sheets every hour to prevent venereal disease . . ."

"Knock it off," O'Neal growled. "This isn't a real vacation. We're here on a mission, remember?"

"Yeah," Fanelli snorted. "A lousy twenty-five grand providing the CIA hasn't fucked up the operation before it began or they don't decide to cheat us on final payment."

"Watch your mouth in public," O'Neal complained. "This may not be the greatest assignment we've ever had, but we're stuck with it. Let's just do the job and get the hell out."

"When are we supposed to meet our contact?" Caine inquired as they took the elevator down.

"That's where we're goin' now," O'Neal answered.

The Hard Corps left the hotel and walked to the Prado. The street was lined with stalls selling fruits, vegetables, and various commodities. Most of the merchants were Indian women dressed in lavish petticoats and bowler der-bies. They've been remarkably successful in this field and many of these shrewd, financially aggressive, and fiercely independent ladies earn more than fifty thousand dollars a year, a very large sum by Bolivian standards.

The mercenaries ignored the merchants and located a small tavern called El Loro Rojo. A faded plywood sign with a crude painting of a scarlet macaw hung above the entrance. The mercs filed through the canvas curtain at the doorway and entered the tavern.

El Loro Rojo was a sleazy little bar with cheap furniture

and dirty walls layered with residue from smoke, dust, and fly dung. Sawdust was strewn across the floor, mingled with spit and cigarette butts. A bored bartender looked up and suddenly smiled when he noticed the newcomers were dressed as Americans. Two young women seated at a table near the door displayed professional smiles and fussed with their hair. Fanelli smiled back at them.

O'Neal scanned the room and found a heavyset man seated at a table in a corner. The guy's reddish-brown hair was thinning at the top and it didn't look as if it had been combed for at least a week. His broad nose had been broken and bent out of shape. Blue blood vessels lined his nose and cheeks. The bottle of whiskey on the table in front of him was half-empty and he was drinking alone.

"I hate to say it," O'Neal muttered, "but that's our contact."

"That drunken slob?" Wentworth asked with a frown. "I've never been terribly impressed by the CIA, but even the Company wouldn't trust somebody like this."

"Why not?" Fanelli grinned. "They trust us, don't they?"

"No more than they have to," Caine spoke, his voice barely above a whisper.

They approached the man at the table. He raised his head and smiled at the mercs. His eyes were only slightly blurred and his hand was fairly steady as he gestured toward the chairs across from his position.

"You gents lookin' for some conversation?" he inquired with a thick Dublin accent. "I speak English if'n that be a consideration."

"How's the Scotch whisky?" O'Neal asked, now aware of the odd code words Saintly had given him.

"The Irish is better," the man answered with a sly grin. "As always. Now we've got the password nonsense outta the way. Me name is Paddy Murphy. Who might you be?"

"If you don't know about us we've got a problem," O'Neal remarked as he joined Murphy at the table. "And if we've got a problem, you've got a bigger one."

"Christ, mate," Murphy replied. "I know why you're here. I was just askin' what your names might be. Don't get your arse in an uproar. Nothin's wrong."

"That's a relief," O'Neal said as he took his cigarettes from a pocket. "I understand you're into guns, Murphy."

"Oh, yes," the Irishman smiled. "I can get you a fine selection of the best weaponry. In fact, your Uncle Samuel is supposed to pay for anything you get. Correct?"

"We're not carrying that much cash," the Hard Corps commander stated. "I understood payment would be handled through a third party."

"That's right," Murphy confirmed. He poured a generous portion of whiskey into his glass. "It's all taken care of. I think we need another bottle here."

"We'll pass on drinks for now," Wentworth told him as he sat at the table.

"I wasn't talkin' about another bottle for *you*," Murphy chuckled as he raised the glass to his lips.

The two prostitutes approached the table. Fanelli was the only man in the group who was intrigued by the pair until he realized they were much younger than they appeared to be at first glance. The elder of the two was probably no more than fourteen. In spite of their makeup and experienced manner, they were still little girls who'd lost their childhood by some cruel twist of fate.

"You no want, señor?" one of the girls pouted. "Is only ten dollars American. Have us both for twenty . . ."

"Not tonight," Fanelli replied as he handed them both a twenty. "This is so you know it's not personal. We just got to have some privacy right now."

"*Sí,*" the hooker smiled. "*Gracias,* señor."

"*Muchas gracias,*" the other added as they shuffled across the room.

Fanelli was embarrassed as he joined the others at the table. "This isn't the time for screwing around anyway, Joe," O'Neal told him. "It's not the time to get shit-face drunk either, Murphy."

"Don't worry," the Irishman assured him as he gulped down the whiskey from his glass. "I can handle it."

"That's what I used to say," Fanelli, the reformed alcoholic, growled under his breath.

"You're also supposed to introduce us to somebody named Garcia," O'Neal reminded Murphy as he grabbed the bottle before the gunrunner could reach for it.

"You'll meet him tomorrow," Murphy declared, glaring at the Hard Corps leader. "We'll all get together at the Plaza Venezuela in front of the old San Francisco Church at noon. I'll introduce you to him then. Now let go of that fuckin' bottle, mate."

"I expect you to stay sober during our mission," O'Neal warned, still holding the bottle. "Drunks tend to talk too much and to the wrong people."

"It's a dangerous thing to come between an Irishman and his whiskey," Murphy warned, fists balled with rage.

"Don't give me that shit," O'Neal snorted. "I'm Irish myself."

"Why didn't you say so?" Murphy grinned. "Let's head over to Club 21. Things don't really start happenin' over there until after midnight, but when they do it's fuckin' great. We'll all get good and drunk and screw our brains out."

"I don't think he's listening too well, Captain," Caine sighed as he leaned his chair back to the wall. "Want me to get his attention?"

"Not in here," O'Neal answered. "Let's not have an incident in a public place. Listen, Murphy—"

The conversation came to a halt as nine men filed into the Red Parrot. They were dressed in ill-treated street clothes with tattered undershirts and black leather vests. Most of them had beards and none had shaved recently. A tall man with a red beret perched on his shaggy head pointed a finger at Murphy and smiled, revealing two steel front teeth.

"Been lookin' for you, man," he announced in broken English. "We gotta have a talk, *cabrón*. This time we talk English so we make it sure you *comprende*. Eh?"

The two whores and most of the other customers quietly slipped out the door. The bartender went into a back room behind the bar. Only the Hard Corps, Paddy Murphy, and the nine newcomers remained.

"Hello, Orlando," Murphy greeted with a nervous smile. "Is something wrong, amigo?"

"*Sí,* you Anglo piece of shit," the man with the steel teeth replied as he reached under his vest and produced a small snub-nosed revolver. "This what is wrong. I pay you fifty thousand pesos and you deliver junk-shit like this."

The gun was a Saturday Night Special by anybody's definition of the term. It appeared to be a cheap copy of a Smith & Wesson. *Very* cheap. The manufacturers had used pot metal instead of steel. The size of the bore suggested the revolver fired .22-caliber ammo, probably the low-powder .22 short rounds to avoid blasting the cheap gun apart the first time it was fired.

"You want ten guns for fifty thousand pesos," Murphy began defensively. "No serial numbers, you say. No way they can be traced, right? What you expect for fifty thousand pesos? Ten Colt Pythons? Browning automatics? You want better guns? Steal some more money so you can pay for something better."

"You cheated me, *cabrón*," Orlando snarled. "You the one gonna pay for that, not me."

He suddenly glared at the Hard Corps as if noticing them for the first time. The four mercenaries were still seated at Murphy's table, apparently undisturbed by the confrontation.

"You hombres better leave here quick," Orlando told them. "Unless you wanna get killed with this Irish pig."

"Take it easy, fella," O'Neal announced as he rose from his chair, the whiskey bottle still in his hands. "This doesn't concern us. We don't intend to get involved in somebody else's problems. Okay?"

"Is okay," Orlando replied with a smile as he lowered the revolver.

Wentworth and Fanelli suddenly bolted from their seats and scooped up the table. They charged forward, using the table as a battering ram. The tabletop slammed into Orlando and sent the hoodlum leader into two of his comrades. All three men fell to the floor with the table sliding across their wiggling bodies.

William O'Neal attacked the closest thug who was still on his feet. The Hard Corps commander swung the whiskey bottle with all his might and brought it crashing down on the startled man's skull. Glass shattered and blood seeped from the hood's lacerated scalp. The Bolivian goon fell to the floor as another flunky reached under his best for a weapon.

O'Neal held the broken bottle by its neck and quickly slashed the jagged end into the man's biceps as he tried to draw the weapon. The hoodlum screamed and another cheap revolver fell from his shaky fingers. O'Neal's left fist crashed into the guy's jaw. He almost followed through with a deadly thrust with the broken bottle. O'Neal didn't want to kill any of Orlando's goons. They were scum and he'd probably be doing the city of La Paz a public service by taking them out, but the Hard Corps didn't want to be in the middle of a homicide investigation before they'd even started to carry out their mission.

He tossed the bottle over his shoulder, throwing it far enough to prevent one of the creeps from picking it up.

O'Neal snap-kicked the wounded man in the lower abdomen. The guy doubled up with a groan and O'Neal clasped his hands together to deliver a powerful chopping blow to the thug's collarbone. A dull crack between shoulder and neck announced that the bone broke. The man groaned and slumped unconscious to the floor.

Steve Caine drew his survival knife and attacked another hoodlum who had just drawn another piece-of-shit snub gun. The sharp steel blade sliced into skin and muscle in the man's forearm, cutting to the bone. The thug howled in agony and dropped his pot-metal piece. Caine raised his knife hand and swiftly hammered the butt of his weapon into the point of his opponent's jaw. The goon moaned softly and fell senseless at Caine's feet.

The metallic click of a switchblade drew Caine's attention. Another hoodlum held a Spanish-made push-button stiletto in his fist. The Bolivian lunged for Caine's belly, weapon held low for a vicious plunge into the merc's intestines.

Caine dodged the attack and swung his survival knife at the Bolivian's weapon. The sawtooth back of Caine's blade struck the switchblade and parried the direction of the enemy's thrust. The hood's arm rose and Caine grabbed the wrist above the switchblade with his left hand.

The mercenary held his opponent's weapon at bay and reversed the grip on the survival knife in his right hand. Caine swiftly rammed the butt of the knife handle into the cluster of nerves at the thug's armpit. The Bolivian gasped as the switchblade fell from his numb fingers. Caine drove the knife handle under the goon's rib cage. The man folded at the middle from the blow and Steve Caine knocked him unconscious with a hard knee-kick to the jaw.

Another Bolivian low-life hood removed a steel pipe cudgel from under his vest. James Wentworth III pounced on the thug before the guy could even raise his pipe club.

Wentworth's hands chopped like twin ax blades across the hood's forearms. The pipe fell harmlessly to the floor. Wentworth delivered a heel-of-the palm blow under the thug's jaw. The guy's head bounced from the blow and Wentworth hooked a hand around the back of his opponent's skull and turned sharply. He bent his knees for leverage and pushed to send the dazed hoodlum hurtling to the floor.

The thug hit the wood surface hard. He started to rise and then slumped on his belly in a gasping heap. However, one of the goons who had been knocked down by the table had recovered enough to jump Wentworth from behind. He wrapped a brawny arm around Wentworth's neck and tried to apply a rear stranglehold.

In the movies, heroes usually escape from this hold by just throwing the strangler over a shoulder. In reality this could result in a broken neck if the guy held on. Wentworth knew better than to try such a move. Instead, he hooked his fingers into the crook of his opponent's elbow to ease the pressure at his throat and reached back with his other hand to grab the guy's hair.

Wentworth stomped a boot heel into the strangler's instep. The man grunted, but held on. Wentworth continued to use one hand to pull at the crook of the guy's elbow while his other hand groped at his opponent's face. His thumb touched the side of the hood's nose and slid a quarter of an inch to jab into an eye.

The Bolivian cried out in pain and alarm, fearful the merc might gouge his eye from its socket. He released his choke hold to protect his face. Wentworth immediately seized the thug's arm with both hands. He twisted the guy's wrist into a lock and braced his other hand against the elbow. Wentworth secured the armlock and rammed a knee into his opponent's chest.

The hoodlum groaned and Wentworth slashed the side of his hand across the base of the man's skull. The thug fell to one knee and Wentworth raised an arm, bent his elbow, and smashed it between the dazed hood's shoulder blades. The goon hit the floor face-first. He didn't utter a sound. Wentworth was convinced the guy was unconscious, but he kicked him behind the ear to make sure.

Joe Fanelli had grabbed a chair and charged at a hoodlum who was trying to draw a snub-nosed revolver. The tough guy from Jersey slammed the chair across his opponent's chest and sent the guy hurtling across the room. The stunned thug fell against the bar and groped for the gun he'd dropped when Fanelli hit him.

The merc lunged with the chair and drove the wooden legs into the hoodlum's torso and groin. The man moaned with pain and Fanelli raised the chair to deliver a short, hard stroke. A chair leg struck his opponent just above the temple. The guy uttered a long "oooh" and dropped senseless to the floor.

Another hoodlum who'd been smacked by the table rose and launched himself at Fanelli. The merc turned to confront the attack, but a solid kick sent the chair flying from his grasp. The thug's hands grabbed Fanelli's throat and he shoved the Hard Corps trooper into the bar. Fanelli's back hit the counter as the Bolivian goon continued to throttle him.

Fanelli's hands rose to clap his open palms across his opponent's ears. The man cried out as an eardrum burst. Fanelli quickly hooked a short, hard right cross to the side of the man's skull. The thug released Fanelli and staggered backward.

Joe jabbed a left to the guy's breastbone and clipped him on the jaw with a right. The thug swayed like a drunkard, but swung a wild punch at his opponent. Fanelli easily dodged the roundhouse right and moved behind the hoodlum. His arms slipped under the armpits of his opponent and his hands clasped at the guy's neck to secure a full-nelson hold. Fanelli shoved his adversary forward and drove him into the bar. He maintained the full-nelson to slam the hood's face into the countertop. The man's body went limp and Fanelli released him and watched the unconscious hood slump to the floor.

Orlando, the gang leader, crawled out from under the table. He was still dazed, but the pot-metal .22 was still in his fist. O'Neal stomped on his wrist to pin the man's gun hand to the floor. Orlando growled like a cornered beast and displayed his two steel front teeth. O'Neal's other foot kicked the revolver out of Orlando's hand. The hoodlum grabbed O'Neal's ankle with his free hand.

"Don't try it," the Hard Corps commander warned. "Unless you want *all* your teeth to be made of metal."

Orlando released O'Neal's ankle and held his hand up in surrender. Paddy Murphy hummed cheerfully as he trotted about the room, gathering up the cheap revolvers and knives dropped by the hoodlums during the battle. Then he strolled to Orlando and kicked the man in the ribs.

"Knock it off!" O'Neal ordered, his eyes glaring at the arms merchant.

"This son of a bitch planned to kill me," Murphy complained.

"I didn't notice you giving us any help while we were fighting these guys to save your ass," the Hard Corps leader snapped. "So back off now."

"I was goin' to help," Murphy said with a shrug. "But you blokes took care of them before I could lend a hand. I'm impressed."

"Wonderful," O'Neal snorted. He removed his foot from Orlando's wrist. "Okay, fella. We're going to leave now. You stay here and look after your man. We were easy on you guys this time. Fuck around with us again and we'll make sure you don't come back a third time."

"*Sí*, señor," Orlando said as he started to rise. "I don't want no more trouble with you."

"Let's go," O'Neal told his teammates.

"Thanks for the exercise," Fanelli told Orlando. "It sure cleared up my jet lag."

"Shut up and come on," O'Neal insisted.

CHAPTER 6

THE SAN FRANCISCO CHURCH was a very old and honored monument to Christianity in La Paz. The white stucco structure, trimmed with red tile, had been lovingly cared for by the faithful. It was a beautiful remnant of another age, and a testament to the ideals and culture that had endured throughout the centuries here in the Andes, despite the political changes and social unrest that had long been part of Bolivia's history.

The Hard Corps stood outside the church, snapping photographs like the other tourists who stood nearby. They mingled with the crowds beneath the morning sky as they waited for Paddy Murphy to join them with DEA agent Victor Garcia. They lingered in the area until a few minutes after noon when the gunrunner finally arrived, accompanied by Garcia.

Victor Garcia was roughly six-and-a-half feet tall with the thickly muscled upper body, narrow waist, and muscular thighs of a pro football player. His features were broad and flat with a high forehead and thick black eyebrows. Garcia wasn't the kind of guy you'd want to meet in a dark alley—unless you happened to be packing a bazooka.

Murphy introduced Garcia to the Hard Corps although he wasn't sure what to call the mercenaries since they hadn't exchanged names yet. The Hard Corps had already come up with a few names for Murphy. The Irish gunrunner hadn't made a favorable impression the night before and they weren't sure they could trust him.

"Paddy tells me you guys are real tigers," Garcia remarked as he shook hands with the Hard Corps members. "That's what my CIA contact told me to expect. Of course he got his information from a secondhand source. Code name 'Saintly'?"

"We know him," O'Neal said with a nod. "Prince of a guy. Practically volunteered us for this mission."

"Glad you weren't crazy enough to ask for it," the DEA agent commented. "I'd have some sincere doubts about your intelligence if you had."

"Maybe we shouldn't discuss this out in the open," Wentworth suggested. He glanced about suspiciously at the tourists and Bolivian passersby.

"Let's get some coffee," Garcia replied. "There's a nice quiet coffee shop on the corner. Shouldn't be very crowded this time of day either."

They followed Garcia to the shop. Dressed in a wool poncho and bowler derby, the DEA agent looked like a native cholo—a person of mixed Indian and Spanish blood. In fact, that was exactly what Victor Garcia was. He had been born and raised in Bolivia before becoming a naturalized U.S. citizen. Garcia ordered coffee for the group, speaking a language he had learned years before acquiring English. The Hard Corps realized they couldn't pretend to be anything except Americans visiting Bolivia. Their appearance, less-than-fluent Spanish, and accent made any attempt to fade into Bolivian society an impossibility. They simply smiled and nodded a lot at the guy behind the counter.

"Could I get some brandy in my coffee?" Paddy Murphy inquired.

"No," O'Neal said sternly. "And you'd better have some decent weapons for us, Murphy."

"Yeah," Fanelli added. "I'm tempted to kick you between the legs just to find out if you have anything there. You sure didn't show much evidence that you've got any balls last night."

"I wasn't carrying a gun," Murphy complained. "Not a good idea for me to carry heat in La Paz. The coppers suspect what I do for a living. I'm a bit past my prime for fightin' with my fists, you know."

"I guess alcohol helps one to pass one's prime a little early," Wentworth muttered.

"That's enough," O'Neal told them. He leaned an elbow on the edge of the table and turned to Garcia. "We were told you'd have a target for us."

"That's right," the DEA agent confirmed. "A major cocaine operation. The leaves are delivered to the site and the *coquitos* process it into coca paste. Easy to do. That part doesn't require any ability for chemistry. Used to be coca paste was either refined into pure cocaine or used here in South America. Addicts here roll cigarettes with coca paste and smoke them for a high."

"Sounds like what they call 'crack' back in the States," Wentworth commented.

"Virtually the same," Garcia confirmed. "Coca paste mixed with baking powder. They call it 'crack' on the East Coast and 'rock cocaine' on the West Coast. It's cheaper than pure cocaine and smoking it can be ten times more potent than snorting regular coke. Addiction can occur real fast. And don't let anybody kid you, cocaine *is* addictive. Physically, mentally, and any other way you want to look at it. Crack has only been popular in the U.S. for a couple of years, but it's rapidly becoming the second most dangerous drug on the illegal market."

"What's number one?" Fanelli inquired. "Heroin?"

"Heroin use hasn't increased much over the last ten

years," Garcia answered. "It has a well-deserved bad reputation and most people don't want to touch it. The number one illegal drug in the U.S. is cocaine—that's the traditional hydrochloride powder cocaine people put up their nose, shoot in their veins, and free-base."

"Are they processing pure cocaine at the site you've chosen for the hit?" Steve Caine asked.

"You bet," Garcia confirmed. "They've got at least one skilled chemist working at the site. Processing coca paste into cocaine requires precise mixing with ether and hydrochloric acid. Those are dangerous chemicals to be screwing around with and a chemist who knows how to handle them safely is worth his weight in gold to the *coquitos*."

"Maybe I'm missing something," Fanelli began. "But the U.S. sent troops to Bolivia to launch raids on centers like the one we're talking about. Why haven't they hit it?"

"Because they haven't been very effective here, that's why," Garcia said with a sigh. "The Administration sends troops down here. The troops are assigned to assist the Leopards—that's what the Bolivian antidrug shock troops like to call themselves—in raids on cocaine processing centers and jungle laboratories. Trouble is, there are people in high positions of authority within the Bolivian army and the central government who are on the take to El Dorado. When the troops and the Leopards learn about a site, somebody usually warns the *coquitos* about a possible raid and by the time the troops arrive, the hoods have disappeared and taken their dope with them."

"That's why they haven't made any big busts?" Wentworth asked.

"The fact they've busted anyone at all is a miracle." Garcia laughed bitterly. "The Americans and the Leopards swoop down on their targets in helicopters. You know how noisy choppers are. In a jungle far from the sounds of traffic and airports, you can hear a chopper coming before it's within twenty kilometers of your site. The smaller jungle labs are designed to take apart and run at a moment's notice. That's why we decided to handle this job differently.''

"We'll need help finding the place," O'Neal stated.

"You'll have it," Garcia assured him. "I'm going with you. El Dorado has started murdering DEA agents. One of the victims was a friend of mine named Rodriguez. I've got a personal score to settle with those bastards.''

"Vengeance and hatred are no match for experience and skill," O'Neal warned. "You have any of the latter?''

"I've been in a few scraps," Garcia answered. "I wasn't exactly raised on a pillow here in Bolivia and I was a cop in the States after I became a U.S. citizen.''

"Cops follow a different rulebook than we do," O'Neal told him. "This is war, Victor. The only rule is to win—any way you can.''

"Don't worry." Garcia smiled. "My morality isn't great enough to cause a problem. I also realize you guys are far more experienced and better trained in this sort of thing than I am. So you're in charge and I take orders from you. Fair enough?''

"We'll need a guide, sir," Caine reminded O'Neal.

"Yeah," the Hard Corps commander agreed. "Okay, Victor. You're in. When are we going to hit the base?''

"As soon as possible," Garcia advised. "The bastards know it's risky to stay set up for too long. Sooner or later, the authorities will learn where they are. Their setup is pretty large so they intend to do business for a while. Trouble is, I don't know how long they've already been in operation.''

"What's the opposition?" O'Neal asked. "How many men does El Dorado have at the base?''

"At least twenty," Garcia answered. "Maybe more. The number can vary according to the amount of work in progress.''

"They're well armed," Murphy remarked, sipping his coffee. The Irishman grimaced at the taste. "The El Dorado gunmen are armed with Uzi submachine guns, Ingrams, M-16 automatic rifles, Winchester pump shotguns, and a variety of handguns. Brownings, Colts, Berettas, Smith & Wesson revolvers . . ."

"How do you know that?" Wentworth demanded.

"I sold the guns to them," Murphy answered with a shrug.

"Figures," O'Neal muttered with disgust. "I hope you're going to supply us as well as you did the opposition."

"You'll get even better weapons," Murphy promised. "And explosives. Composition Four, RDX compound. Are you familiar with it?"

"Yeah," Fanelli, the team demolitions expert, confirmed. "I've used it lots of times. Hope you've got some special blasting caps and primacord. You can't detonate C-4 with the number sixes used for dynamite."

"That's taken care of," Murphy assured him.

"Hey, Murphy," O'Neal began. "You've got connections with El Dorado. You wouldn't have them for customers otherwise."

"I just sell guns," Murphy answered. "I'm not responsible for what folks use them for."

"A legal firearms dealer doesn't sell weapons to gangsters if he knows that's what they are," Wentworth remarked. "But then, you don't have any principles. Do you, Murphy?"

"I see." Murphy smiled. "You're worried about Victor because he might be too moral, and me because I might not be moral enough. Odd concerns for a bunch of blokes who make their living by killing other people. You're mercenaries, right? Hired killers for anybody who can pay your price."

"You're wrong about that," O'Neal told him. "We choose our assignments and who we'll work for carefully.

We won't take on any mission that could hurt the interests of the United States or help tyrants, gangsters, or totalitarian governments. But, we don't care if you're an opportunist, Murphy. Unless you decide to contact your pals in El Dorado and warn them we're coming, that is.''

"Why would I do that?" the gunrunner demanded, a trace of outrage in his voice. "The *coquitos* wouldn't exactly reward me for helping you out and in order to tip them off I'd have to admit my part in this.''

"You could tell them you sold guns to us and later found out what we planned to do,'' Wentworth stated. "El Dorado would believe that since you don't care who you sell arms to. They'd probably reward you for protecting them under those circumstances.''

"Well, I guess you'll just have to trust me,'' Murphy sneered. "Won't you?''

"We trust you,'' O'Neal told him. "As long as we can keep an eye on you. Guess what that means, Murphy? You're coming with us.''

"What?'' the Irishman glared at the Hard Corps leader. "That's not part of the bloody deal, damn it! I just supply the weapons. I don't go mucking about shooting people or getting shot at . . .''

"You're coming with us,'' O'Neal repeated in a hard voice. "I figure if your ass is on the line you won't betray us or give us a bunch of crap to fight El Dorado with.''

"I won't do it!'' Murphy declared as he started to rise from his chair.

Fanelli and Caine stood. Both men stared into the gunrunner's eyes, their expressions grim. Caine eased a hand toward the inside of his jacket, toward the survival knife at the small of his spine. Fanelli placed a fist into his other palm and cracked his knuckles. Murphy decided it was in his best interest to return to his seat.

"What if I don't tell you where the guns are?'' he asked after a moment's pause.

"I think I can get you to tell us," Caine said with a cold smile. "Amazing what sort of information I can get from a man after a couple of hours. All I need is a campfire, a sharp knife, and someplace where the guy can scream his lungs out without anybody hearing him."

"I know a place you can use," Victor Garcia commented.

"Don't help these lunatics!" Murphy snapped.

"Their mission is virtually the same as mine," Garcia said with a shrug. "You're only interested in making a buck, Paddy. Same as you used to before you had to leave Ireland."

"Something we should know?" O'Neal asked, raising an eyebrow.

"You want to tell them or should I?" Garcia asked Murphy.

"Fuck you, Victor," the Irishman growled. "Okay. I sold guns in Ireland. Sold weapons to the IRA and to the Protestant militants. Each side found out I was supplying their enemies, so I decided it was time to move on."

"I wondered what an Irishman was doing in Bolivia selling arms," Wentworth remarked. "I guess you figured Latin America offered a good market for your business."

"Lots of would-be revolutionaries and terrorist groups," Fanelli added. "Keeps a fellow like Paddy pretty busy."

"Don't lecture me," Murphy growled. "I'm going with you on the raid. What more do you want?"

"We want you to stay with us," O'Neal told him. "You're going back to the hotel with us and we're going to get some 'camping gear.' Then we'll meet Garcia and you'll take us to the guns. No bullshit, Murphy. You'll take us to the guns and then we go directly to the El Dorado base."

"And when do we start all this?" Murphy asked, although he suspected the answer wouldn't make him happy.

"Right now," O'Neal replied. He turned to Garcia. "Is that okay with you?"

"No problem," the DEA agent assured him. "I can be ready in less than an hour. You guys are running this show. Should I contact the CIA at the embassy and let them know we're about to move out?"

"Hell no," O'Neal told him. "What they don't know they can't screw up for us. We'll let them know when the job's over. They might be pissed off that we didn't keep them fully informed, but they'll still be happy to hear the mission was a success so they can start taking credit for it."

"What if it isn't a success?" Garcia wondered out loud.

"If we fail we'll probably all be dead," Wentworth informed him. "So what difference will it make whether the Company is upset or not?"

"Sure won't make much difference to us," Fanelli added with a fatalistic shrug.

CHAPTER 7

THE EL DORADO base was located near Bolivia's western border twenty kilometers from the point where Bolivia, Peru, and Chile meet. The cocaine gangsters had chosen a site at the base of a mountain, flanked by several other mountains. It was virtually impossible to find from the air since planes wouldn't ordinarily fly low enough to pass between the mountains, especially when clouds and mist reduced visibility.

The Hard Corps, Victor Garcia, and Paddy Murphy traveled up to the pass in two army-surplus Jeeps. They parked the vehicles as the terrain became more difficult and continued to trek on foot to the enemy base. All six men wore loose-fitting fatigue-style shirts, trousers, and boots. They were well-armed, carrying weapons and ammunition supplied by Murphy.

The gunrunner hadn't sold them junk. O'Neal, Fanelli, and Murphy were armed with Uzi submachine guns. Wentworth, Caine, and Garcia carried M-16 rifles. All six men also had 9-mm Browning autoloading pistols, machetes, and hand grenades. O'Neal and Wentworth carried Bushnell binoculars around their necks.

Steve Caine had brought a hunting bow with a seventy-five-pound pull and a quiver of hunting arrows among his "camping equipment." The quiet mercenary had learned the deadly archery skills of the Katu during his years with the tribe. Caine favored the bow for taking out opponents from a distance when silence and a lack of muzzle flash was advantageous.

Garcia led the group along the mountain pass. The Bolivian-born DEA agent was familiar with this part of the Andes, and he easily hiked along the rugged path. The four Hard Corps men were in superb physical condition and had no trouble keeping up with Garcia, thanks to the extra red blood cell injections they had received before leaving the States. Murphy had been living in Bolivia long enough to adjust to the altitude, but he was in poor shape from his alcohol-soaked life-style. The Irishman huffed and puffed as he brought up the rear.

"For Christ's sake," Murphy complained. "Can't we slow down? What's the rush for? I thought you wanted to hit El Dorado after dark. It isn't even sunset yet . . ."

"Watch your mouth," O'Neal warned in a harsh whisper. "Sound can travel a long way in the mountains. We have to hurry because we don't have any night-vision gear. Maybe you don't mind attacking an enemy site where we're outnumbered more than two to one without trying to learn as much as possible about the setup first, but the idea doesn't appeal to the rest of us."

"We're getting closer," Garcia announced in a soft voice. "Listen."

Latin music was playing faintly in the distance. The Hard Corps smiled. El Dorado was overconfident. Their security was obviously pretty sloppy because somebody was playing a radio loud enough to be heard more than three kilometers away. But then, the *coquitos* didn't have any reason to expect trouble. Their location protected them from aerial discovery and the rocky pathways were only traveled by *peones* and nomadic Indians.

The music became louder as the Hard Corps group drew

closer to the site. They traveled two-and-a-half kilometers, favoring the shadows and boulders for cover in case El Dorado had lookouts posted. At last the mercenaries were within view of the enemy base.

Four canvas tents were set up in the center of the enemy camp. Several figures moved about within the base. O'Neal raised his binoculars to his eyes and adjusted the focus knob, taking care to shield the lenses from the sunlight to prevent reflections on glass from flashing a telltale warning to the *coquitos*.

The magnified view of the camp came into focus. Two gunmen, armed with submachine guns, paced along the rim of the camp. Both men carried binoculars slung from their necks, but neither seemed to feel a need to scan the surroundings for possible danger.

Still, the Hard Corps couldn't afford to underestimate their opponents. The sentries didn't pose much of a challenge, but the camp was populated by almost two dozen *coquitos* and most carried weapons. They huddled around a campfire, drinking rum-laced tea to ward off the chill as a cold wind moved in from the north. Others supervised a number of workers who were mixing coca leaves with kerosene. Another trio of gunmen watched *peones* straining cheesecloth containing coca leaves that had already been soaked in kerosene.

O'Neal noticed that the peasants didn't appear to be willing employees. The workers shuffled about slowly, their heads hung low. Their clothing was ragged and the *peones* seemed to be overworked and underfed. Most of the *coquitos* appeared to be Bolivians of Spanish descent or cholos of mixed Spanish and Indian blood. But, the *peones'* dark skin and features suggested they were Indians from villages around the area.

"What the hell's going on there?" Wentworth muttered as he peered through his binoculars. "Looks like slave labor."

"Yeah," O'Neal replied softly as he trained his field glasses on the largest tent in the enemy compound.

The canvas flap was drawn back to expose several large jars that contained a milky white substance. Portions of the contents sparkled as if diamonds had been mixed in with the thick liquid. O'Neal suspected what the jars contained, but he handed his binoculars to Garcia to have the DEA agent confirm his notion.

"Cocaine," Garcia whispered. "That's the chemist's tent. The coca paste has been mixed with hydrochloric acid and ether. What settles at the bottom of those jars will be pure cocaine. See how it shines? Must be very pure stuff. Worth close to a thousand dollars an ounce on the street in the States."

"How you want to handle this, Bill?" Wentworth looked at O'Neal as they ducked behind a boulder. "Just want to destroy the coke and let the *coquitos* go?"

"I'm not sure any of us can legally arrest them," Garcia commented. "That means we either kill them or let them go."

"If they run, let 'em go," O'Neal decided. "If they try to fight, kill 'em. Do your best to avoid hitting any of those poor devils they've forced into slave labor. I doubt if any of them will try to defend the *coquitos,* but if they do we'll have to burn them too."

"Big talk," Paddy Murphy snorted. "But how do you plan to get close enough to take them out?"

"Steve?" O'Neal began, turning to Caine. "I think you know what to do."

"Yeah," Caine replied quietly, handing his M-16 to O'Neal. "I'll take care of the sentries. Might need some backup after I do it. Not a hell of a lot of cover between the sentries and the camp. Pretty good chance somebody will see me take them out."

"We'll take care of that," O'Neal assured him. He tossed the M-16 to Wentworth. "You and Murphy will cover us from the rear. Put the rifles on semiauto. We'll want precise shooting so we don't wind up getting hit by friendly fire.''

"Okay," Wentworth replied as he checked the selector switch of the weapon. It was on safety. He figured it could stay there until the rifle was needed. "And I'll keep an eye on our Irish friend in case he decides to switch sides."

"Oh, bloody hell," Murphy growled.

"I'm serious, Murphy," Wentworth warned the gunrunner. "If I even suspect you're up to anything I'll blow your brains out."

"Okay," O'Neal continued. "Steve takes point. Joe and Victor will go in from the east. Ordinarily I'd have Victor stay farther from the front, but we might need you to translate and to warn the Indian slaves that we're not after them. You speak their lingo, right?"

"I don't know," Garcia said with a shrug. "How the hell do I know what sort of Indians they might be?"

"Do the best you can," O'Neal urged. "I'll take up the west flank. The mountains will block them off to the north and Jim and Murphy will have the south covered. Any questions?"

"Did any of your mothers have any idea who your fathers might be?" Murphy asked with a disgusted sneer.

"How'd you like a machete blade for an enema?" Fanelli hissed at the Irishman.

"Come on," O'Neal ordered. "The sun's setting and we've got work to do."

"Hey," Garcia began, an urgent tone to his whispered voice. "Don't forget they've got ether in the chemist's tent. That stuff can be ignited by a single spark and it's very explosive. If it goes up, it'll take about half the camp with it. Maybe more. We can't be sure how much they've got stored in there."

"Now ain't that a shame," Fanelli said with a grin. "After all, nobody wants to get blown to bits."

"Always seemed like a natural fear to me," Garcia replied. "That's why I'm worried about the ether tanks in that tent."

"And you can bet the *coquitos* are worried about it, too," the Hard Corps demolitions man said thoughtfully. "They might even be more worried about it than we are."

"You have an idea, Joe?" O'Neal inquired.

"Just thought of something that might give us an extra edge, Captain," Fanelli answered. "The enemy knows what's in that tent, but they *don't* know that *we* know it, too."

"Yeah." O'Neal smiled and nodded. "I see what you mean."

Twilight descended upon the Andes. The flames of the campfire illuminated the El Dorado camp in a flickering yellow glow. The *coquitos* turned on diesel-powered generators, which provided electricity for the lights in the tents, as well as the sunlamps trained on the kerosene-soaked coca leaves. A cook was preparing dinner. The guards were relieved of duty and two new sentries took over.

Steve Caine silently crept toward the rim of the camp. His face and hands were covered by dark brown camouflage paint so that he could blend into the shadows and surrounding rock walls. He held his hunting bow low in his left hand. The quiver of arrows was attached to his belt at his right hip. His Browning 9-mm pistol was in a shoulder holster under his right arm and his survival knife was sheathed in a cross-draw position at his belly. Caine's right hand was fisted around the handle of a machete with a thick, two-foot-long black blade.

The big jungle knives had been brought along in case they encountered dense foliage or needed a chopping tool that could serve as a weapon in an emergency. None of the

Hard Corps team had needed to use their machetes thus far, but Caine recognized the heavy blade and sharp edge of the big knife made it ideal for sentry removal.

He slithered between the rocks, creeping through the darkness like a low shadow. His progress was slow, but he knew that people are less apt to see something in the dark if the object doesn't appear to move. Slowly, Caine drew closer to the first sentry.

Caine smiled thinly, lips pressed tightly together to conceal his teeth. He watched the unsuspecting guard through slitted eyelids. The *coquito* was armed with a submachine gun that resembled a Beretta M-12, but he was more interested in trying to peak into the open flap of a tent than watching the area surrounding the camp.

The guard actually turned his back to Caine as he tried to get a better look inside the tent. The Hard Corps merc wondered what was going on inside the tent that intrigued the guy so much. Caine heard voices whistling and whooping in a vulgar manner from the camp. Flickering, multicolored light pulsated within the tent that had captured the guard's attention.

As Caine gazed across the camp to make certain no one was looking in his direction, he glimpsed inside the tent and saw the answer to the mystery. The *coquitos* had set up a large-screen television inside that tent. The TV was powered by the diesel generators and it was apparently connected to a video-cassette tape player. Nearly half the *coquitos* had crowded inside the tent to watch a pornographic movie, which featured a bondage scene involving barbed wire. Caine figured anybody who found something that sick sexually stimulating probably deserved to die.

He swiftly rose up behind the unsuspecting guard and swung his machete. The man gasped at the moment the heavy blade struck the top of his skull. Perhaps he had sensed Caine's presence a split second before the sharp metal cleaved through bone and sank deep into his brain.

The sentry died instantly. Caine yanked the handle of his machete and pulled the corpse to the ground. The blade was still lodged in the dead man's head.

"Gonzales?" a voice called from within the camp. "*¿Que hace usted?*"

Caine froze in a low crouch beside the slain victim. The other sentry at the opposite side of the camp had noticed sudden movement at the first guard's position. He obviously hadn't seen Caine take the guy out because he was asking what Gonzales was doing. The merc eased an arrow from the quiver on his belt as the second sentry moved closer.

"Gonzales?" the man called out again and switched on a flashlight.

The beam fell across Steve Caine and the dead guard. The sentry's mouth open in astonishment and terror when he saw the bow in Caine's left fist. The merc had drawn back the bowstring with his right hand. His fingers released the arrow notched to the string. The bow hummed softly and fired its missile with a sharp hiss.

The arrow struck the guard under the breastbone, left of center. The steel broadhead pierced flesh and bit upward into the man's heart. The *coquito* sentry uttered an ugly groan of pain and tumbled to the ground. The beam of his flashlight whirled around the camp as the torch rolled beside the twitching corpse.

Alarmed voices near the campfire warned Caine that this time the other El Dorado goons were aware one of their comrades had been cut down. Caine dashed for the cover of a trio of boulders as flashlight beams streaked after him. The Katu-trained merc drew back the bow with a fresh arrow already notched. He kept running as he turned and fired the arrow at the closest flashlight.

A scream revealed that the arrow had struck the *coquito* behind the flashlight. Caine didn't waste time congratulating himself on his archery skills as he scrambled behind the boulders. A barrage of automatic fire erupted from the El Dorado gunmen. Bullets ricocheted against the stone surface of Caine's shelter as the merc ducked low and removed a grenade from his belt.

The *coquitos* charged from tents and darted about the site. Four thugs were still firing at the boulders where Caine was holed up. William O'Neal saw the situation as he moved in from the west. The Hard Corps leader crawled forward with his Uzi cradled across his elbows. He held his fire until he was within effective range.

One of the hoods who was trying to gun down Caine suddenly fell backward, a subgun still gripped in his fists. A bullet hole formed a small scarlet eye in his forehead. The other *coquitos* failed to notice the report of James Wentworth's M-16 amid the roar of automatic weapons. The Hard Corps second-in-command calmly selected another target. The sights of his rifle centered on the forehead of an El Dorado hitman. Wentworth squeezed the trigger again and watched the man's face disappear in a spray of crimson.

Someone noticed the muzzle flash of Wentworth's weapon. A salvo of automatic fire streaked toward the general vicinity of the lieutenant's position. Wentworth had already ducked. Paddy Murphy hugged earth near the mercenary's post. The Irishman cursed under his breath as a hailstorm of high-velocity bullets passed over them.

"Bloody wonderful!" Murphy cried sarcastically. "And just what the bleedin' hell are we supposed to do now?"

"Wait our turn," Wentworth replied as he sprawled into a prone stance and dug in his boots for a firm anchor.

O'Neal opened fire with his Uzi. The 9-mm parabellum rounds raked the gunmen who still threatened Steve Caine. Bullets smashed into the *coquitos'* torsos. Their bodies twitched and jumped from the impact. Two enemies collapsed while another dropped to one knee, blood oozing from a bullet wound in his chest. The guy still tried to point his Ingram machine pistol toward O'Neal's position.

The Hard Corps leader triggered another burst of Uzi slugs. Parabellums ripped into the *coquito*'s throat, shattered neck vertebrae, and transformed his face into blood-splashed pulp. The hoodlum fell beside his slain comrades as O'Neal fired into another group of opponents. Uzi rounds tore into one flunky's rib cage and sent him hurtling into another pair of *coquitos*. A fourth El Dorado buttonman doubled up in a moaning ball as he clutched his bullet-punctured belly. His forehead touched the ground as if in genuflection. This would have been an appropriate gesture since the man was about to die.

Joe Fanelli and Victor Garcia appeared at the east end of camp, near the chemistry tent. Garcia opened fire with his Uzi and pumped automatic rounds into a pair of *coquitos* who were trying to seek safety in the wrong direction.

Fanelli cocked back an arm and lobbed a grenade through the open flap of the chemistry tent. Terrified voices cried out from inside the tent, and three men swiftly bolted into the open. Only one man carried a gun and he didn't even try to fire at any of the Hard Corps raiders. The other two were middle-aged and paunchy. The disgruntled chemists followed their panic-stricken bodyguard, running with admirable speed considering their age and poor physical condition.

With a satisfied chuckle, Joe Fanelli dashed toward the tent. Garcia followed, still firing his Uzi into the El Dorado gang. Both men slipped inside the tent. Fanelli scooped up the grenade he'd previously tossed into it. The *coquitos* had been too scared to notice the pin was still in the grenade. Fanelli attached the weapon to his belt and smiled at Garcia.

"Told you it would work," he told the DEA agent.

"You said it had a fifty-fifty chance," Garcia growled as he inspected the cocaine laboratory.

"Well," Fanelli said with a shrug. "I was at least fifty percent right then."

Fanelli whistled softly as he glanced over the bottles of hydrochloric acid and ether in the El Dorado lab. They had gallons of the stuff stored at the base. Quickly, he examined the coke in the big jars. Each container was big enough to hold at least twenty gallons and there were ten full jars in the tent. The milky contents possessed a strangely tranquil beauty with the gemlike sparkle of the substance; it reminded Fanelli of morning snow reflecting the light of the sun.

"God," Garcia commented as he shook his head with dismay. "They must be turning out nearly a hundred kilos a day from this place."

"Not anymore," Fanelli said in a matter-of-fact voice.

A *coquito* gunman appeared at the mouth of the tent. The thug pointed his MT-12 at the pair, but held his fire as he stared at the array of chemicals on the shelves. He had obviously been warned about the volatile nature of the substances and didn't want to fire at the intruders for fear of blowing himself up.

Fanelli didn't hesitate. The merc fired his Uzi from the hip. Three 9-mm slugs sent the gunman sprawling backward to crash to the ground, blood spewing from a bullet wound in the heart. Fanelli barely glanced at the corpse as he opened a canvas pack on his belt and removed some C-4 plastic explosive.

"Jesus Christ," Garcia rasped, gazing at the ether bottles. "You could have blown us all to bits, Joe!"

"Calculated risk," Fanelli replied with a shrug. The demolitions expert was accustomed to handling materials that could blast him to eternity and he accepted the risk as easily as most people accept the possibility they might have a car accident on their way home from work. "We're still here, aren't we?"

"I almost had a heart attack, but I guess I'm okay," the

DEA agent commented as he watched Fanelli insert some primacord into a small chunk of C-4. "What are you doing?"

"Making sure nobody tries to haul ass with this coke," the merc answered, moving to the jars of hydrochloride cocaine in the final process. "Watch the entrance, Vic. Don't give 'em a clear target. Hopefully nobody's gonna be too eager to pump bullets into the tent, so you oughta be safe as long as you don't expose yourself."

"I hope none of the *coquitos* are as crazy as you are," Garcia muttered as he stepped to the mouth of the tent and peered outside.

"That's not very likely," Fanelli replied cheerfully.

The Hard Corps merc fitted a special blasting cap to the explosives and attached an igniting device to the wires. The contraption was pressure controlled. The plate was braced under one of the heavy jars. If the jar was moved, pressure would be taken from the plate and the C-4 would explode.

"Company's coming," Garcia warned as he saw several El Dorado gunmen head toward the tent. However, as Fanelli predicted, the enemy goons were afraid to fire at the tent because of the danger of igniting the chemicals within.

"Okay," Fanelli said, stepping away from the cocaine. "Let's use the back door."

"There isn't any—" Garcia began as he glanced about at the canvas walls of the tent. "I get it."

Garcia drew his machete from its sheath and headed to the opposite side of the tent. He swung the big knife in a two-hand overhead sweep. The blade slashed through canvas to cut a long rip in the wall. Garcia pushed through the hole and stepped outside.

"¡Manos arriba!" an enemy gunman snarled as he pointed his Ingram MAC-10 at the DEA agent.

Another *coquito* stood beside the guy with the machine

pistol. He held a .45-caliber Government Colt in his fists, also aimed at Garcia. The DEA agent raised his hands slowly, the machete still clenched in his right fist.

Fanelli had heard the voice ordering Garcia to raise his hands. An El Dorado hitter had gotten the drop on Garcia, Fanelli realized. He aimed his Uzi at the canvas, pointing the barrel in the direction of the *coquito*'s voice. The muzzle nearly touched the canvas. Fanelli squeezed the trigger.

Parabellum rounds punched through the tent and tore into the two gunmen on the opposite side of the canvas. Two bullets slammed into the guy with the Ingram. Copper-jacketed missiles ripped muscle from the *coquito*'s right deltoid and bored an abrupt tunnel in the side of his jawbone. The hinges splintered and teeth rolled loose inside his mouth. The bullet tore an exit wound at the hood's cheekbone on the opposite side of his face. He dropped his MAC-10 and fainted.

The other *coquito* had received a 9-mm slug in the right biceps. He cried out in pain and staggered from the impact of the high-velocity projectile, which burned through muscle and chopped into bone. Yet, he managed to hold onto his .45 pistol.

Garcia's arm suddenly snapped forward and the machete flew from his fingers. The muscular DEA agent threw the jungle knife hard. The heavy blade struck the *coquito* in the chest. The point pierced his breastbone and the sharp edge sank into flesh to cut across the aorta. The major artery to the left ventricle of the man's heart was severed. He tumbled to the ground and vomited almost a pint-and-a-half of blood before he died.

Fanelli emerged from the slit in the canvas, his Uzi held ready. Garcia nodded his thanks to the merc and walked to the corpse with the jungle knife still lodged in his chest. The DEA agent placed a foot on the dead man and grabbed the handle of his machete. A hard yank pulled the blade from the lifeless flesh.

The pair darted behind the other tents, rapidly moving toward the Indian slaves at the section of the camp where coca leaves were processed. Most of the El Dorado thugs were unaware Fanelli and Garcia had penetrated the base. The *coquitos* were still busy exchanging shots with O'Neal at the west end and Wentworth and Murphy to the south.

Three El Dorado killers had remained close to the Indian forced laborers, apparently concerned that the slaves might take advantage of the raid to try to escape. The *peones* had dropped to the ground and hugged the earth, waiting for the fighting to end one way or the other. The trio of *coquito* keepers saw Fanelli and Garcia approach. The thugs raised their weapons.

Fanelli sprayed two opponents with the remaining rounds left in his Uzi. Bullets slammed into the gunmen and sent their bleeding bodies tumbling across the terrified Indians who cowered helpless on the ground. Garcia's subgun roared and stitched the third *coquito* with a line of bullet holes from right hip to left shoulder. The guy went down without managing to fire a single round from his Brazilian-made MT-12.

"Try to communicate with these fellas," Fanelli told Garcia as he swapped magazines to reload his Uzi. "Tell them we're not here to hurt 'em and we intend to free them."

"Okay," Garcia replied as he lowered his weapon and approached the Indian workers.

Fanelli watched for possible threats from the remaining *coquitos* while Garcia spoke with the prisoners. The DEA agent stared at the iron manacles locked to the ankles of every Indian laborer. The chain between each man's ankles was only a foot long. The Indians couldn't make a run for it if they tried. "These folks aren't going anywhere," Garcia announced.

"Neither are we right now," Fanelli replied as he aimed his Uzi at a pair of *coquitos* headed toward their position.

*   *   *

The El Dorado hoodlums had virtually forgotten about Steve Caine during the firefight. The bearded mercenary remained behind the boulders with a hand grenade in his fist in case his position was overrun by the enemy and he would be forced to make a final deadly gesture to take as many *coquitos* as possible with him to the grave.

However, Caine was no longer the center of attention and he took advantage of the distraction caused by the shooting done by his teammates. The merc put the grenade back in his belt, and crept from his shelter with his bow slung over his shoulder. Caine moved to the corpse of the first sentry he'd taken out. The machete was still jammed in the dead man's skull.

Caine ignored the jungle knife and relieved the corpse of a compact submachine gun. The sentry's weapon was an MT-12, the Brazilian version of the Beretta M-12. Caine had handled the M-12 before and the MT-12 was virtually identical to its Italian counterpart. He worked the bolt to be certain there was a round in the chamber and stealthily slipped into the heart of the enemy base.

A sharp-eyed *coquito* noticed Caine melt into the shadows. The hood swung his CAR-15 toward the elusive merc's position. William O'Neal saw his pal was in trouble and fired a trio of Uzi rounds into the chest of the would-be ambusher. The *coquito* fell lifeless to the ground and Caine continued to move farther behind enemy lines.

Caine trod across the corpses of two slain El Dorado flunkies as he moved behind a tent. The merc listened by the canvas structure, but didn't hear any voices or movement within the tent. He drew his survival knife and slit a hole in the canvas to peer inside. The tent was deserted, but Caine found the interior intriguing nonetheless.

Three steamer trunks were lined along the canvas walls. A television set was perched on one trunk, a ham radio and an IBM computer terminal were mounted on the others.

Near the center of the tent stood a card table covered with white silk. China plates and crystal glasses were set up for a single person. Whoever the tent belonged to, the owner clearly ranked high on the El Dorado chain of command.

Amid the gunfire within the battlefield, Caine heard an engine growl as it protested starting up. The sound didn't belong to a diesel generator, Caine suspected. He guessed it was a car engine. The sound guided Caine to an area near the mountain base where El Dorado had parked a trio of military-style two-ton trucks.

Two men were in the tractor section of one of the trucks. The rig rolled forward on thick, reinforced rubber tires. Caine quickly rushed the truck and raised his MT-12. He triggered the subgun and raked a fast volley of 9-mm rounds across the hood and windshield of the enemy vehicle.

A couple of bullets pierced the metal skin of the hood. Several others smashed the windshield to bits. Chunks of glass hurtled from the shattered window. At least one bullet struck the man behind the steering wheel. The driver slumped forward and his head leaned on the horn at the center of the steering wheel. The monotonous single note of the truck horn blared with a long, continuous bellow.

The door at the passenger side popped open. A youthful figure jumped behind the truck hood for cover. Dressed in a white silk shirt and matching trousers, the guy realized he couldn't blend into the darkness well enough to escape. He used the hood for a bench rest and aimed a Beretta .380 pistol at Caine's position.

The Hard Corps merc triggered another volley of 9-mm slugs at the lone gunman. Bullets sparked against metal and the *coquito* in white ducked behind his cover. Caine immediately dashed to the front of the vehicle and dove headlong to the ground.

Caine fell to earth and ducked his head to execute a rapid forward roll. The momentum carried Caine past the front bumper to the other side of the truck. He landed in a sitting position directly in front of the startled El Dorado ringleader.

Caine's MT-12 was already trained on his opponent as the *coquito* tried to aim his Beretta at Caine. The Brazilian subgun erupted first. Patches of blood seeped from the man's chest. Crimson-dyed spots appeared on the man's white shirt. The gunman's body slid along the length of the truck hood and fell lifeless near the left-hand tire.

A black attaché case lay near the still body of the dead sub-chief. Caine gathered up the briefcase and knelt beside the white-and-red-clad corpse. The merc used the thick blade of his survival knife to pry open the lid to the case. Several packets of white powder tumbled from the case. Caine dumped the rest of the contents. He didn't have the time to count them, but there must have been over twenty packets in all, each containing roughly one-fourth of a kilo. Apparently the El Dorado team leader had decided to grab some of the purest coke before he tried to escape the carnage.

"This crap isn't going anywhere," Caine remarked, glancing down at the cocaine packets. "And neither are most of the *coquitos*."

He gathered up the coke as quickly as he could and tossed it into the back of the truck. The mercenary found a can of gasoline at the motor pool and poured the contents over the truck. Caine dragged the dead man away from the vehicle before he removed the matches from the survival gear in the hollow handle of his knife. He struck a match and set fire to the gasoline.

Flames quickly spread across the vehicle. Caine hurried from the truck. The fire soon covered the rig and ignited the fuel tank. It exploded, blasting the truck into a billowing cloud of scrap metal.

The fiery wreckage scattered across the camp and further disoriented and demoralized the *coquitos*. Fanelli and

Garcia remained by the Indian prisoners and fired at the El Dorado forces while O'Neal and Caine hit the enemy with a crossfire at the west. Wentworth and Murphy continued to pick off opponents with carefully aimed sniper fire.

El Dorado wasn't used to fighting adversaries who struck with such force and cunning. A few survivors realized they were no match for the Hard Corps. They bolted on foot from the campsite. Wentworth tracked them through the sights of his M-16, but held his fire. None of them carried rifles and only one was armed with an automatic weapon—a short-range Ingram. The group of escapees wouldn't try to ambush the Hard Corps without any long-range weapons. Wentworth decided there was no need to kill them.

Murphy's M-16 snarled with a burst of full-auto fire. The Irish gunrunner had also noticed the fleeing *coquitos*, but he didn't feel as generous as the merc lieutenant. Three 5.56-mm rounds tore into the back of the hood with the Ingram. Murphy watched the man fall and quickly fired another volley between the shoulder blades of another El Dorado goon.

"That's enough," Wentworth ordered, deflecting the barrel of Murphy's weapon by knocking it toward the sky with his own M-16.

"What the hell?" the Irishman barked. "Are you crazy?"

"Let's just say I don't hold with shooting men in the back unless there's enough reason to justify it," the Hard Corps officer replied. "Blame it on the Southern code of chivalry I was raised with."

"Bloody stupid to let them get away because you suddenly decided to get honorable," Murphy complained.

"They're no threat to us now," Wentworth insisted. "So forget about them."

An angry battle cry drew their attention to four *coquitos* who had suddenly charged straight for their position. Two opponents were armed with submachine guns. The third carried a rifle and the fourth appeared to be armed only with a machete.

Wentworth turned to face the attackers and fired his M-16 from the hip. A bullet slammed into the face of the nearest *coquito*. The slug tore through the bridge of his nose and ripped a path in his brain before exiting at the back of his skull.

Murphy's '16 blasted a trio of 5.56-mm rounds into the chest of the next attacker. The man's feet left the ground and his body slammed to earth hard. The third *coquito* tried to aim his Uzi at the Irishman. Murphy's rifle spoke once more and fired the last two rounds from the magazine. The *coquito* screamed and whirled about from the impact. The submachine gun sprang from his grasp, but the Bolivian hitman bellowed with rage and charged toward Murphy as he reached for a sheath knife on his belt.

"Fuck you," the Irishman muttered, drawing a Browning 9-mm pistol from the holster on his hip.

Murphy shot the guy in the belly. The *coquito* staggered and fell to one knee. The gunrunner aimed his pistol with both hands and pumped another round into the top of his opponent's skull. A large portion of the man's head vanished in a shower of brains and bone fragments. His corpse flopped on its back in a spread-eagle pose.

The fourth attacker kept coming, machete held overhead in both fists. Wentworth stepped forward to meet his opponent. The lieutenant held the M-16 in his left hand while his right rested on the hilt of the machete in a cross-draw position on his belt.

The *coquito* swung his jungle knife. Wentworth raised the M-16 and blocked his opponent's blade with the steel barrel. The merc swiftly drew his own machete in an *iaijutsu* "lightning draw." Trained in Japanese fencing, Wentworth stepped forward with the motion of the cross-body slash he delivered to the *coquito*'s abdomen. The blade cut a deep, long wound in the Bolivian's belly.

Wentworth stepped to the side of his opponent as the thug doubled up in agony, immediately terminating the man's suffering with a machete stroke to the back of the *coquito*'s head. The sharp blade split skull bone and bit into the guy's brain. Wentworth yanked the knife free and allowed the dead man to fall face-first to the ground.

An unexpected explosion startled Wentworth and Murphy. They dropped to the ground and covered their heads as the violent eruption echoed along the rock walls. A fireball rose from the enemy base. Smoke and burning debris were all that remained of the tent that had been used by the El Dorado chemists.

"I think somebody found my booby trap!" Fanelli's voice called out happily from the remnants of the campsite.

"No shit!" Murphy shouted in reply, his body trembling with the aftereffects of tension.

CHAPTER 8

"WELL," WILLIAM O'NEAL began as he surveyed the charred wreckage and mangled corpses after the battle was over. "I'd say this is one cocaine-processing center that is definitely out of business."

"Unless there's some sort of profit to be made by selling burned canvas scraps," Wentworth commented, stomping out some flames from a ragged piece of a demolished tent.

"Did Murphy behave for you?" O'Neal inquired.

"No complaints," Wentworth said with a shrug. "Murphy did his share. Took out eight *coquitos*. A couple of those weren't necessary. He shot them in the back while they were running away. Still, he was competent with a rifle and didn't try to run out on us."

"That's all that matters," O'Neal stated, lighting up a cigarette. "We don't have to like Murphy. When this mission is over, we'll never have to set eyes on the bastard again."

"Another reason to be glad when this is finished," Wentworth remarked. "And we've done what the CIA sent us here to do. We found a big cocaine center, crushed it, and destroyed the dope. Now we can go home and go back to working for ourselves again."

"Yeah," O'Neal agreed, but his voice betrayed concern. "Only thing is, we're not out of Bolivia yet."

"Hey, gentlemen!" Victor Garcia announced as he approached the two Hard Corps officers. "I just set fire to the coca paste using the kerosene that survived the battle. Must have been close to a hundred kilos of the stuff. Joe's booby-trap bomb destroyed the processed coke in the jars. That had to be another hundred keys. I haven't taken a body count yet, but I'd say we took out nearly forty El Dorado enforcers. Not a bad night's work."

"I hope the Company will be as pleased about it as you are," O'Neal said. "What's the story on those Indians who appeared to be slave labor for the *coquitos*?"

"That's exactly what they were, Captain," Joe Fanelli announced as he joined the others. "El Dorado had even put chains on the poor bastards. Couldn't find the keys to their manacles, but a chisel and a rock worked almost as well. We freed 'em and let 'em go home."

"El Dorado had abducted them from the Indian villages up in the mountains," Garcia explained. "Apparently this has been going on for some time, but the villagers were afraid to report it because the *coquitos* threatened to kill the prisoners if anybody squealed on them. The Indians have always gotten the shit end of the stick ever since the days of the conquistadores. They lose their land, become second-class citizens in their own country, and wind up doing slave labor. Used to be they were forced to work on plantations and tin mines. Now it's cocaine."

"I hope they can get back to their villages on their own," O'Neal said. "We don't have room in our jeeps to provide cab service."

"They can manage," Garcia assured him. "The Indians know this area like you know the block you live on. They can find their way home and they know how to live off the land until they do. They're very grateful to you guys for rescuing them."

"Wasn't part of our job," O'Neal said with a shrug. "But we won't charge extra for it."

"That's wonderful," Murphy snorted as he stepped forward. "Now that we've done a good deed and made your Yank government happy, may we get the hell out of here?"

"Before we leave," Steve Caine began as he approached the others, dragging a corpse by an ankle, "you guys might want to take a look at this."

"What you do, Steve?" Fanelli asked, glancing down at the dead man. The corpse was that of the young man in the white short-sleeved silk shirt and white linen trousers. "Kill an ice cream man?"

"He must have specialized in snowcones," Caine replied. "The guy was carrying a briefcase full of cocaine in little baggies. About ten keys. I burned the coke and blew up the truck this bastard was trying to escape in. I think this character was the head *coquito* at this camp."

The others gazed down at the dead man. The gangster must have been no older than twenty-five. A pencil-thin mustache extended across his upper lip, but his jaw and cheeks had recently been shaved. A tiny gold cross hung from a golden chain around his neck. The bottom of the cross was round. It was actually a miniature spoon, just the right size to sample cocaine.

"Pretty young to be in charge of a big operation like this place was," Wentworth remarked, finding nothing else of particular interest about the dead man.

"Son of a bitch," Garcia rasped as he stared down at the dead man's face. "This is Alberto Juarez."

"It *was* Alberto Juarez," Fanelli corrected.

"Was he somebody important?" O'Neal inquired.

"Little Alberto was the son of Cesar Juarez," Garcia explained. "Deputy Minister of Justice Juarez. A high official in the Bolivian central government, well connected with the army and most of the major police departments throughout the country.''

"Oh, shit," O'Neal muttered as he tossed down his cigarette next to the corpse. He angrily ground it out under his boot. "Are you sure about this guy?"

"I'm sure about Alberto *and* Cesar Juarez," the DEA agent insisted. "We've had the deputy minister under surveillance for some time. DEA has suspected the senior Juarez was on the take and secretly working for El Dorado, but we were never able to come up with solid proof to convince the Bolivian government to arrest him. Needless to say, the central government isn't about to take action against one of their own without some real hard evidence. We also suspected Alberto was working for El Dorado, but we figured he was probably just a go-between. Apparently, the kid ranked pretty high in the organization.''

"So what's the big deal?" Fanelli asked with a shrug. "Alberto was caught red-handed. You got the proof you need and now you DEA guys can go after his dad—"

"Maybe you forgot something, Joseph," Wentworth began as if speaking to a mentally slow child. "We're not supposed to be here. Remember? This whole mission has no official sanction by either the Bolivian or U.S. government. We can't go to the authorities and neither can Victor.''

"We'd better dispose of Alberto's body," O'Neal declared.

"What good is that going to do?" Murphy demanded. "Thanks to the Southern-fried moralist you straddled me with, three *coquitos* managed to escape. I would have stopped them, but Rhett Butler here objected to me shootin' them in the back.''

"I've always found cold-blooded murder to be distasteful," Wentworth remarked, glaring at the Irishman.

"Not sporting, eh?" Murphy sneered. "If I'd've been allowed to stop those bastards we wouldn't have to worry about them reporting the incident to El Dorado. They'll surely tell the other *coquitos* that Alberto Juarez was among the casualties. That news will reach the deputy minister and we're all going to be in very deep shit.''

"Why?'' Fanelli wondered out loud. "Nobody knows we hit the place.''

"I'll fall under suspicion,'' Garcia remarked. "The Bolivians are always suspicious of DEA agents who aren't working directly with them twenty-four hours a day. They'll also be looking for Paddy because everybody in La Paz knows he's one of the biggest gunrunners in Bolivia. We had to get the weapons somewhere and Paddy will be a Number-One source under suspicion.''

"That means our cover is pretty weak,'' O'Neal said grimly. "A dozen people saw us at the Red Parrot with Murphy. Somebody is bound to remember us, because we got in a fight with a bunch of punks. Wonderful situation.''

"How do we handle it?'' Wentworth asked.

"I could try to track down the three *coquitos* who escaped,'' Caine suggested. "I might be able to find them before they can reach a radio or telephone.''

"Too risky,'' O'Neal replied. "Those guys know this area a lot better than we do. You can read sign better than anyone I know, Steve, but even you'll have trouble tracking in the dark. Trying to hunt them down would probably be a waste of time.''

"So what do we do, Captain?'' Fanelli asked.

"Get rid of Alberto's body,'' O'Neal insisted. "We'll bury it and cover the grave with rocks or something. If the authorities don't find the body right away, Deputy Minister Juarez might figure his son managed to escape or that we took him prisoner. That'll slow him down a bit.''

"Why don't we just leave his body for them to find?'' Wentworth suggested. "If the authorities find Alberto's corpse among the *coquitos* they'll realize he was connected with El Dorado and maybe they'll go after the old man . . .''

"Fat fuckin' chance," Fanelli said, clucking his tongue with disgust. "Alberto's father is a bigwig in the central government. He'll cover up for his kid and probably come up with some sort of bullshit that Alberto was kidnapped by El Dorado and murdered by a rival gang which attacked the base and probably ripped off the original hoods."

"I am aware of the fact that you still regard the police with the mentality of a juvenile delinquent from Jersey," Wentworth said stiffly. "And your lack of respect for authority nearly got you kicked out of the army. But this imagined conspiracy by the Bolivian authorities is pure paranoia—"

"I'm afraid it isn't," Garcia interjected. "Not the way things work here in Bolivia. Government officials can get away with just about anything, and a man in Juarez's position can get lots of soldiers and cops to help with a cover-up."

"Then it's settled," O'Neal said sternly. "We get rid of Alberto's body. Then we head for the nearest town or city with telephone lines and Victor calls somebody in DEA or CIA. Let them know we accomplished the mission, but we can't leave Bolivia via commercial airliner as previously planned. Tell them they'd better help us get the fuck out of here because it'll be one hell of a scandal if we get arrested and talk to the police. Or the Bolivian feds."

"Think they'll go for it?" Wentworth asked.

"They'd better," O'Neal replied. "I don't care to spend the rest of my life in a South American prison."

CHAPTER 9

THE HARD CORPS, Victor Garcia, and Paddy Murphy approached the city of Corocoro a few minutes after daybreak. They decided to get rid of the Jeeps before entering the city. If either the Bolivian authorities or El Dorado found the tire tracks near the site of the previous night's battle, the stalkers would easily be able to identify the vehicles used by the raiders as two military-style Jeeps. Anyone looking for the mercenary team in Corocoro wouldn't have much trouble if the residents recalled seeing half a dozen men ride into the city in two army Jeeps.

They also had to get rid of most of their weapons. The Uzis and M-16 rifles were too obvious and suspicious. The Hard Corps and their two allies only kept the Browning pistols, extra magazines, and one hundred rounds of 9-mm for each man. Fanelli kept half a pound of C-4 concealed in a coffee can. They also held on to their machetes, but wrapped the jungle knives in canvas to disguise the weapons. Caine used a similar trick to conceal his hunting bow and quiver of arrows. He still carried his pet survival knife in a sheath at the small of his back.

The mercs and their companions walked to the city limits of Corocoro. It was considerably smaller than La Paz, with few big buildings, poorly paved roads, and

93

practically no traffic at that early hour of the morning. A pair of farmers drove a donkey-drawn cart along the street. Some early workers pedaled bicycles past the cart. Only two cars and a battered old truck passed within view of the Hard Corps.

Corocoro wasn't popular with tourists and the hotels usually had plenty of vacancies. The Hard Corps found a place called La Casa de Corocoro, which rented rooms for five bucks a night. They checked into the rooms and left most of their gear hidden under beds. Then they headed for a small diner across the street.

"What are we going to do after breakfast?" Murphy asked, chewing an omelet as he spoke. "Go shopping for souvenirs?"

"No," O'Neal answered. "We're going to buy some new clothes. Stuff that looks more civilian. Then Vic needs to find a public phone and make some calls."

"I still don't see why you insisted that we stay at a hotel," Murphy complained. "If they're looking for us in La Paz, they'll be looking for us here too."

"The first thing the authorities or El Dorado will do is watch the airlines and possibly the main roads that extend across the borders of Peru and Chile. Of course, they may have no idea who we are and it will probably take a while for them to figure it out. We could head for La Paz and try to flee the country before they start checking passengers, but my guess is they'll be suspicious of anybody who traveled from the United States and decided to leave Bolivia after only being here for three days."

"That's only true about you four gents," Murphy said smugly.

"You think a noted gunrunner like you wouldn't be nailed as soon as he showed his face in La Paz?" Wentworth asked with a smile. "You're in even worse trouble than we are, Murphy."

"Bastards ruined my business," the Irishman snorted. "What the hell am I supposed to do now?"

"That's your problem," O'Neal said without sympathy.

"Actually there's no way anyone can prove we were responsible for the incident," Garcia remarked, hoping no one would disagree.

"There are traces of cordite on our hands and probably on our skin and hair as well," Wentworth reminded the DEA agent. "A paraffin test would prove that we had fired weapons less than twenty-four hours ago. Unless we can convince the authorities that we all just happened to come across some automatic weapons and decided to do some harmless target shooting and then we lost the guns before we could report them to the cops, I think a paraffin test would give them enough evidence to put us in jail for a while. It wouldn't take much longer for them to come up with enough evidence to *keep* us there."

"We'll only stay in Corocoro for a day or two," O'Neal explained. "We're staying at the hotel because that's where tourists would stay. And we're going to act like tourists while we're in town. Take pictures and hang around the more colorful places in this lively town. Don't do anything suspicious and stay out of trouble."

"That'll be easy enough," Fanelli commented. "What's the hard part?"

"With a little luck," O'Neal replied, "maybe there won't be any."

"I have a suggestion, Bill," Wentworth announced. "We should split up into pairs. That way, if the Bolivian feds or the *coquitos* are looking for us, they won't find six men together. They'll be less inclined to suspect us if we're not all bunched together."

"Two guys won't be able to defend themselves as well as six," Fanelli reminded the others. "Ever hear of divide and conquer?"

"That's a risk we have to accept," O'Neal stated with a shrug. "Splitting up in pairs leaves each group more vulnerable, but it increases the odds for the others to get away. The advantages outweigh the drawbacks.''

"Okay," Fanelli agreed reluctantly. "Who goes with who?"

"I've spent enough time with Murphy," Wentworth complained. "Let somebody else put up with him for a while."

"Joe, you go with Murphy," O'Neal instructed. "Jim will go with Steve and I'll tag along with Victor. We'll meet at the hotel at twenty-one hundred hours."

"Huh?" Murphy seemed confused.

"Nine o'clock tonight," Caine translated for the gunrunner. "If you forget, Joe will remind you."

A young Indian approached the group. He wore a wool poncho and held a wide-brim hat in his hands. The Hard Corps pretended to ignore him, but they watched the youth carefully from the corners of their eyes. The Indian might be harmless, perhaps a beggar or a lad looking for work as a guide. But greed is a universal character trait and members of virtually every ethnic group and more than a dozen nationalities are involved in the cocaine trade. It was possible the youth worked for El Dorado.

"Excuse me," he began in a shy voice although his English seemed very good. "My name is Raul Metza. I would like to talk with you, please."

"This is a private party," Murphy said gruffly.

"Just make it brief, kid," O'Neal added, wondering if the young Indian might know something of value.

"I spoke to someone who told me about you," Raul explained. "He told me how you six men rescued him and several others who were forced to work for El Dorado. He told me you killed many *coquitos* . . ."

"Your friend made a mistake," O'Neal told him. "We're just tourists."

"He is afraid to speak with you because he thinks El Dorado will be looking for you," Raul continued. "But when he told me of your courage and skill, I knew I had to speak with you. My village needs your help.''

''I suggest you ask the police or the government to help,'' O'Neal said. ''We're just passing through and we need to be at the airport to get our flight back to Santa Cruz. You're talking to the wrong guys, fella.''

''My village is poor,'' Raul began, ''but we will pay you as much as we can—''

''Look,'' O'Neal said sharply. ''I don't want to be rude about this, but I've already told you we're not going to get involved in your village or its problems.''

''I'm sure you have your reasons, señor,'' Raul said, unable to conceal the disappointment from his expression. *''Vaya con Dios.''*

''Same to you, kid,'' O'Neal replied.

They watched Raul shuffle across the street. His head hung low and his arms dangled uselessly. He appeared to be spiritually crushed by their rejection.

''You were a little hard on him, sir,'' Steve Caine remarked. He rarely criticized the Hard Corps commander, but Raul had touched a sympathetic nerve. Caine felt the Indians were similar to the Katu he'd known so well in Vietnam.

''I was blunt,'' O'Neal corrected. ''We don't have time to spare crusading for oppressed villages. It would have been worse if I'd built up the kid's hope. We can't get involved, Steve. We've got enough troubles of our own.''

''Now that's what I call an understatement,'' Fanelli said with a sigh.

CHAPTER 10

"OH, FOR CHRIST'S sake," Paddy Murphy complained, pouring himself another glass of whiskey. "Have a bloody drink, Joe, or whatever your name really is. A man can't celebrate properly with goddamn soda pop."

"I told you I can't drink, damn it," Fanelli replied sourly as he watched the Irishman gulp down his fourth shot of whiskey.

Joe Fanelli wished he hadn't agreed to enter the tavern with Murphy, but the gunrunner had insisted that hanging out in bars was a perfectly natural activity for tourists. He'd also told Fanelli that they could probably find some women in the tavern. That excuse had convinced Fanelli that spending some time in the bar might not be such a bad idea.

However, there were no women in the tavern. Four other men customers were present and none of them seemed to be looking for female companionship. Murphy had urged Fanelli to be patient. Nearly an hour had passed and no women had entered the drab little bar. Fanelli was bored as he sipped lukewarm soft drinks and watched Murphy quaff booze.

"You think you're too good to drink with me?" Murphy demanded. "I expected that from those two snotty officers, but not from a trooper. One little drink isn't going to hurt you.''

''I quit drinking about ten years ago,'' Fanelli replied.

''Then it's about time you had one,'' Murphy insisted, his voice slightly slurred. The Irishman poured whiskey into Fanelli's glass. ''Come on, Joe. You can't toast with an Irishman unless you drink something proper. A good man's drink. Soda is for bleedin' kids, mate.''

''Well.'' Fanelli stared at his glass. The amber liquid seemed very inviting. He picked up the glass. ''Maybe just one.''

''That's my lad.'' Murphy smiled and raised his glass. ''Here's to kickin' arse and makin' money.''

Fanelli sipped the whiskey. The liquid burned a bit in his throat, yet his taste buds relished the almost forgotten sensation of alcohol. A warm glow caressed his belly. Fanelli drank some more. The alcohol rapidly took effect. Despite the synthetic blood used to boost the merc's resistance to altitude sickness, the thin mountain air contributed to his inability to handle liquor. Besides, an alcoholic is always an alcoholic. The cravings can be repressed, but they never really go away.

Murphy poured more whiskey in Fanelli's glass. The Hard Corps merc hesitated, but raised the drink to his lips. He gulped down the third drink without even token reluctance. Murphy slapped him on the shoulder.

''Good man!'' the gunrunner said with a drunken smile. ''Now we can have a good time like a pair of real men.''

''Sure,'' Fanelli replied. The room seemed slightly lopsided, but Fanelli didn't worry about it as he reached for the bottle. Tensions and worries were drifting away in an alcoholic blur and Fanelli felt relaxed and giddy.

''We need another bottle,'' the Irishman decided as he rose from his chair and walked unsteadily toward the bar.

The pair sat at the table, drinking whiskey and exchanging jokes and old war stories, which included more bullshit with each new tale since each man was trying to outdo the other. After an hour or so, they began singing. Murphy favored old Irish ballads while Fanelli liked limericks with plenty of four-letter words.

Neither man paid much attention to the three miners who marched into the bar. They were larger and more muscular than most Bolivians. They also didn't seem to care much for norteamericanos or Europeans. None of them understood English, but they recognized the language spoken by Murphy and Fanelli, and they didn't like the sound of it. To them, English was the language of the powerful tin companies they worked hard for, with so little reward. They stared at the two gringos as they gulped down dark beer from thick glass mugs. Fanelli and Murphy ignored the miners.

"*¡Hijos de las putas!*" the largest miner shouted as he stepped forward and tossed the contents of his beer mug at the two English-speaking customers.

Beer splashed across the tabletop. Liquid splattered Fanelli and Murphy. The Irishman cursed and Fanelli turned to stare up at the three miners. They approached the table. The big guy waved his empty mug and sneered at Fanelli.

"Yeah," the merc growled as he gathered up his glass with one hand and grabbed the whiskey bottle by its neck with the other. "Fuck you too!"

He suddenly hurled the glass at the big miner's face. The contents splashed into the man's eyes and mouth as he tried to dodge the projectile. The glass bounced against the side of his skull. Fanelli bolted from his chair and swiftly kicked the big miner between the legs. The man howled in agony and doubled up with a groan as one of his pals lunged at Fanelli.

The Hard Corps merc clubbed the attacker's closest arm aside with the bottle and quickly jabbed the bottom into the man's jaw. The miner staggered backward from the blow, but the third aggressor seized Fanelli's arm and twisted the bottle from his grasp.

Murphy slammed a fist into the miner's face. The fingers slipped from Fanelli's arm. Paddy Murphy and the third man collided in a clumsy wrestling match as the big miner charged at Fanelli with both arms outstretched.

The merc delivered a left jab to his opponent's breastbone and swung a right uppercut for the larger man's jaw. The second punch missed because alcohol distorted Fanelli's sense of distance. The big man swung a fist into Fanelli's face. The impact sent Joe hurtling backward to tumble over the tabletop and land gracelessly on the floor.

Murphy managed to knee his opponent in the balls and hammered him across the nape of the neck with a fist. The miner fell to all fours and Murphy prepared to hit him again. Another opponent punched the Irishman in the mouth and knocked him to the floor. Murphy landed near Fanelli.

"I think they're getting tired," Fanelli commented, rubbing his sore jaw as he started to rise.

"Oh, yeah?" the Irishman replied, blood oozing from a split lip. "I hope they know that . . ."

The three miners closed in. The big guy and one of his pals moved toward Fanelli while the third man attacked Murphy. The Irishman rose from the floor and rammed his head into the miner's belly. Both men stumbled across the room toward the bar.

The large man reached down to grab Fanelli. The merc braced his back and shoulders against the floor and lashed out with a boot. The kick smashed the miner's nose into a bloody smear and knocked him off-balance to land on his backside.

The big miner's companion raised a foot and aimed a vicious stomp for Fanelli's head. The merc dodged the boot. The guy's heel struck the floor less than an inch from Fanelli's right ear. His arms streaked out and seized his opponent's leg in a flash. Fanelli turned sharply, twisting the miner's leg to throw the man off-balance.

Fanelli jumped to his feet as his opponent started to rise. He slammed a solid right cross to the miner's face. The man fell to all fours. Fanelli stomped on the miner's left hand, crushing bones under his boot heel. The man cried out in pain. The Hard Corps merc silenced the miner with a rabbit punch behind the ear that rendered him senseless.

Strong arms encircled Fanelli's chest. The big miner had attacked from the rear and attempted to apply a bear hug. Fanelli grabbed the man's wrists and thrust the back of a heel between his opponent's legs. The miner groaned in agony when a second kick to his genitals sent a wave of pain quivering through his body.

Fanelli held the dazed man's wrists and raised his arms overhead. The merc bent his knees and folded at the middle to haul the miner onto his back. Then he straightened his legs and ducked forward to send the larger man hurtling overhead in a "flying mare." The big miner hit the top of the table. The wooden legs snapped and both man and furniture collapsed to the floor.

Murphy was still struggling with his opponent. The Irishman swung a wild right at the miner's head. The other man ducked beneath Murphy's whirling fist and rammed a hard uppercut to the gunrunner's stomach. Murphy's belly was full of whiskey and rebelled from the blow. He opened his mouth and abruptly threw up on the miner's shirtfront.

"!Qué chigado!" the miner exclaimed with disgust as he pushed Murphy away.

Fanelli swiftly rushed forward and drove a hard punch to the point of the last opponent's jaw. The man's head recoiled from the blow and his body slumped unconscious to the floor. Fanelli sighed with relief, but a hand suddenly seized his shoulder and started to spin him around.

The mercenary turned with the motion and swung his left fist into the face of the man who'd grabbed him from behind. A green cap hopped into the air as the guy's head bounced. Fanelli gasped with surprise when he noticed the badge pinned to the man's chest.

The police officer fell against another cop. Half a dozen policemen had arrived at the tavern. Fanelli raised his hands in surrender when he saw two of the cops draw their pistols. A couple of others raised their batons.

"Uh . . ." Fanelli began awkwardly, "it was an accident."

A nightstick rapped against the side of his skull and a black veil fell across Fanelli's consciousness.

CHAPTER 11

WILLIAM O'NEAL WASN'T happy about the way things were going. Victor Garcia had managed to contact a CIA case officer in La Paz. The Bolivian government had already learned about the attack on the cocaine base in the Andes. Deputy Minister Juarez was especially upset by this "gang warfare" and claimed that the killers involved would have to be hunted down and brought to justice as soon as possible because such "violent and well-armed assassins pose a greater threat to the safety of honest civilians than the *coquitos* they murdered."

Now wasn't the time to covertly let the government know that Uncle Sam had struck back at El Dorado for killing DEA agents in the past. Juarez was receiving limited support with his mad-dogs-on-the-loose campaign, but support would increase if the central government learned the CIA had sent in a team of mercenaries without any legal status in Bolivia. Nobody cares to have a foreign nation meddling in domestic concerns, even if the meddling nation has a reason to take action and only strikes at criminal outfits.

The Company had claimed they'd be unable to arrange any sort of exfiltration by air until the rainy season ended because fog cover had become too thick for smaller air-

craft to safely travel an unauthorized route. Too dangerous, O'Neal thought sourly. What the hell does the CIA
think our situation is? Of course, he already knew the
answer: it wasn't the Company's problem. However, the
case officer promised that they'd do something as soon as
possible.

To compound O'Neal's chagrin, Fanelli and Murphy
had failed to join the others at the hotel by 2100 hours.
James Wentworth and Steve Caine had arrived right on
time. O'Neal and Garcia had arrived an hour early. What
the hell had happened to Fanelli and the Irish gunrunner?

"It's nine-thirty," Garcia announced, glancing at his
wristwatch. "How much longer we are going to wait for
them?"

"You in a hurry to go somewhere tonight?" Steve
Caine asked as he sat cross-legged on the floor of the hotel
room.

"I'm not in a hurry to be arrested by the feds or
ambushed by El Dorado," the DEA agent answered. "And
there's a pretty good chance one or the other happened to
Paddy and your friend."

"Joe is probably bouncing in a bed with a local tart,"
Wentworth commented as the mahogany swagger stick
rested against his open palm. He'd purchased the stick
from a novelty shop and he was still getting used to its
"feel." "He's been in heat since before the mission started.
Not surprising if he lost track of time under these
circumstances."

"I don't think that's what happened," Caine said softly.
"Joe likes to fool around, but he wouldn't get that careless
in the middle of a mission."

"I agree," O'Neal replied. "Joe and Murphy must have
gotten into some kind of trouble."

"Hey," Garcia began. "I'm not saying we should run
out on them, but you fellas said one reason for splitting up

in pairs was to prevent all of us from getting captured or killed."

"Before we decide what action to take," O'Neal began, "we're going to try to find out what happened to our teammates. If it's humanly possible, we'll get them out of whatever mess they may be in."

A knock at the door surprised the men. Wentworth and Caine reached under the mattress of the bed and extracted four 9-mm Browning pistols. They tossed two guns to O'Neal and Garcia. The Hard Corps commander moved to the door while Wentworth and Caine crouched behind the bed and a chest of drawers. Garcia followed their example and stepped into the closet, pistol held ready.

"¿Quién es?" O'Neal called through the closed door.

"Raul Metza," a voice replied. "We met earlier today."

"I remember," O'Neal assured him. "What do you want?"

"Two of your friends are in trouble, señor."

"Just a minute," O'Neal cut him off. The Hard Corps leader unlocked the door and stepped back, putting his fist holding the Browning behind his back. "Okay. Come in."

Raul Metza opened the door. He was alone and didn't appear to be armed. Entering the room, he gasped with alarm when he noticed the pistols held by the other members of the team.

"I won't tell you not to be afraid," O'Neal said, tucking his weapon under his belt at the small of his back, "because maybe you should be if you're involved in anything that's happened to our friends."

"I was involved in nothing, señor," Raul assured him. "But I saw what happened. About an hour ago, the police arrested them for brawling in a tavern. I think one of them struck a police officer. They are certainly in jail now."

"Oh, fuck," O'Neal groaned.

"Hold on," Wentworth said suspiciously. "How did you know where to find us, Raul?"

"I didn't," the young Indian answered. "That is why it took me so long to locate you. I've been running all over the city checking places where I thought you might be. Then, I remembered that this hotel is across the street from the café where we met. I simply bribed the desk clerk and he told me the room numbers you're staying at."

"Jesus," Garcia rasped. "If this kid can find us that easy, imagine how little trouble El Dorado or the feds would have if they came after us."

"Watch what you say in front of the kid," O'Neal warned. He took out his cigarettes and turned to Raul. "We told you to go to hell earlier. Why are you trying to help us now?"

"Because I still hope to convince you to help my village," Raul admitted. "I will help you rescue your friends if you agree to help my people."

"Is this village very far from here?" Wentworth asked. "Is it in a remote area pretty far from the major cities?"

"I—I'm afraid it is, señor," Raul confessed, fearful that he'd lost any hope of hiring the Hard Corps.

"Sounds like it might be a good place for us to go until we can arrange safe transport out of Bolivia," Wentworth mused. "What do you think, Bill?"

"I think we can make a deal, Raul," O'Neal told the youth.

CHAPTER 12

THE POLICE STATION wasn't very large or impressive by standards in the United States, but Corocoro wasn't a hick town in a TV sitcom. The cop station was made of solid brick and mortar. Several squad cars were parked in the lot and the Hard Corps figured there could be more than fifty cops in the building.

The mercenaries and their allies had little time to check out the station and compose a plan of action, but they came up with a plan based on what they saw of the outside of the building and could guess about the interior. A hundred things could go wrong with their scheme, but the situation was desperate and demanded immediate action regardless of risk.

Steve Caine and Victor Garcia stole a truck, an old Chevy pickup. They parked the vehicle near the police station. O'Neal, Wentworth, and Raul Metza were waiting for them to arrive. The Hard Corps commander and his executive officer were dressed in gray business suits and neckties. Caine and Garcia wore wool ponchos and hats similar to Raul's clothing.

"Where'd you find the truck?" Wentworth asked as he examined the Chevy. It was at least thirty years old. "In a time warp?"

"They don't make 'em like this anymore," Garcia declared, patting the hood of the Chevy.

"I think they passed safety laws to make sure of that," Wentworth said dryly.

"It's the best we could find," Caine said in an apologetic tone. "Wish we could have found something better."

"It'll have to do," O'Neal said with a shrug. "Okay. Everybody knows what to do. Jim and I will go in first. The rest of you guys wait two minutes before you move out."

"Two minutes," Caine said with a nod.

O'Neal and Wentworth walked to the entrance of the police station, both carrying black attaché cases. The Hard Corps officers entered the building. A desk sergeant looked up at the pair, eyebrows raised and the corners of his mouth turned down in an exaggerated frown.

"*¡Habla inglés?*" O'Neal demanded, tugging a lapel of his jacket as he spoke. "We need someone here who speaks English, damn it."

"*Un momento*, señor," the sergeant replied as he picked up a telephone receiver and dialed a single number.

The desk cop spoke briefly into the phone. He barely hung up before a policeman in a cheap brown suit stepped into the lobby. The plainclothesman smiled weakly and approached the two Americans.

"Hello," he began. "I am Detective Sergeant Miguel Veaga. What can I do for you?"

"My name is Griswald," O'Neal answered, flashing an ID folder. It only contained an international driver's license under another phony name, but he tried to prevent giving Veaga a good look at the card. "I'm with the United States embassy in La Paz. Department of State. This is Saul Rosenberg, attorney-at-law and legal advisor for embassy operations."

"Pleased to meet you, Lieutenant," Wentworth announced, saluting with the swagger stick in his right hand.

"Lovely country you have here. Laws are a bit confused, but then that's true just about everywhere."

"We understand you arrested two American citizens for brawling or drunk-and-disorderly or something like that," O'Neal added. "We've come to have a chat with them."

"They were arrested for creating a public disturbance, destruction of private property, assaulting four Bolivian citizens—including a police officer—and resisting arrest," Veaga stated. "That's not including public drunkenness, which would be simply a fine. Your two countrymen are in quite a bit of trouble."

"Idiot tourists," O'Neal growled. "Still, the embassy is expected to look into these matters. You know how that is. Americans travel to other nations and think they can do any damn thing they please. Personally, I say they should let the local authorities handle these situations. Perhaps they would if one of the men wasn't related to a senator from Delaware."

"Delaware?" Veaga frowned. "That's in the United States?"

"More or less," Wentworth remarked.

"I'm not certain the two men we arrested tonight are the same men you seek," the cop told them. "Neither one of them have been very cooperative and one man claims to be an Australian and seems to want us to deport him."

"Sounds like Durkan's idea of a joke," O'Neal said, shaking his head. "Damn fool doesn't seem to realize he's in trouble."

"Then he is either very stupid or he has a very strange sense of humor," Veaga commented.

"Can you arrange for us to speak with the prisoners, Lieutenant?" Wentworth inquired.

"I'm a sergeant, not a lieutenant," Veaga answered. "And I'll have to get permission from my superiors."

"Fair enough," O'Neal assured him.

Caine, Garcia, and Raul entered the station. The tall,

bearded mercenary stood with his back to a wall and the brim of a hat pulled low over his face. Garcia and Raul spoke with the cops in rapid-fire Spanish. They were talking too fast for O'Neal to keep up with his limited Spanish vocabulary, but the Hard Corps commander had helped them come up with the script for the scene.

The DEA agent and the Indian youth were telling the police that they'd been ripped off. The desk sergeant rolled his eyes with frustration and urged them to calm down and explain what happened. Detective Veaga had an errand to do and decided this was an apt time to do it and avoid getting involved in the new crisis that had charged into the station.

The desk sergeant was trying to write down Garcia and Raul's statements, a task made more difficult as both men kept contradicting the other's remarks. O'Neal and Wentworth stepped farther away from the others, as if fearful of getting fleas from the newcomers. Two minutes later, Veaga returned.

"The officer in charge has given permission for you to meet with the prisoners," Veaga announced. "However, we'll have to frisk you both. Standard procedure. You understand?"

"Frankly, I find it rather offensive," O'Neal complained. "But I suppose we'll just have to go along with the rules."

He placed his case on the desk and unsnapped the lid. The desk sergeant muttered something under his breath, probably annoyed because the valise was in the way of his paperwork. O'Neal opened the case and showed the contents to Veaga. The detective glanced at the notebook, pens, and small cassette tape recorder inside the valise.

"That's fine," Veaga sighed. "But we really don't wish to conduct searches here in the lobby, Señor Griswald."

"Oh," O'Neal said with a shrug. "Sorry."

He closed his briefcase and pulled it from the desk top.

Wentworth stood behind O'Neal and placed his valise on
the floor near the merc commander's feet. Garcia, Raul,
and Caine crowded around them and complained to the
desk sergeant—except for Caine, who simply repeated
"por favor" four times and then switched to *"sí, sí"* as if
agreeing with the others.

The confusion distracted Veaga and the desk cop while
O'Neal placed his briefcase next to Wentworth's valise.
He grasped the handle of Wentworth's case and raised it
from the floor. Wentworth grabbed O'Neal's valise, completing the switch.

"Will you gentlemen please come with me?" Veaga
urged, gesturing at O'Neal and Wentworth.

"Did you bring your tape recorder?" Wentworth asked.

"Yes," the team leader answered. "Why?"

"That means we'll have a complete record of whatever
my potential clients have to say," Wentworth replied as he
shoved a briefcase across the desk to the sergeant. "No
need for me to take this in there. Mind looking after it,
señor?"

The desk sergeant glared at Wentworth and growled
something under his breath, but he stuffed the briefcase
under his desk. O'Neal and Wentworth followed Veaga
into a corridor and two doors down to a small conference
room. Two cops were waiting for them.

The policemen frisked the merc officers, checking for
weapons in ankle holsters or hidden in the small of their
backs. They searched for knives or guns strapped to forearms or concealed at the nape of a neck. They checked
every pocket and asked the Hard Corps men to remove
their shoes. One cop fumbled with the combination lock to
the briefcase O'Neal had carried into the room. The merc
officers held their breath.

Veaga spoke to the cop in curt Spanish. The man nodded and stepped away from the valise. Apparently Veaga
had told him it wasn't necessary to check the case because

'he'd already looked inside it. O'Neal and Wentworth managed to exhale without uttering a collective sigh of relief. They had an emergency plan if the valise switch failed, but it would have been even more risky than how they intended to handle the situation.

"I'm sorry, sir," Veaga began, turning to Wentworth. "I must ask you to give me that stick."

"Oh?" Wentworth smiled as he handed the cop his swagger stick. "No problem. Just a silly habit I picked up as a JAG officer in the army. I first practiced law in the service. The old UCMJ was quite a bit different from civilian law."

"UCMJ?" Veaga wondered aloud. "The U.S. Marine Corps?"

"That's the USMC," Wentworth explained. "The UCMJ is the Uniformed Code for Military Justice. It's only used in the military courtrooms and the administrations of commanding officers in the service."

"Must be very interesting," Veaga remarked without much enthusiasm. "I'll go get your countrymen."

He left O'Neal and Wentworth with a single uniformed cop for company. Veaga returned less than a minute later with Joe Fanelli, Paddy Murphy, and a short, balding Bolivian cop dressed in a sweat-stained white shirt and suit trousers. He also wore a shoulder-holster rig, but the holster was empty. Police might carry guns when they interrogate suspects in the movies, but in real life it's considered a serious security risk. Not that the police at the Corocoro station deserved any high marks for maintaining security.

"My name is Lieutenant Morales," the bald man announced in rather choppy English. "Sergeant Veaga tells me you're with the United States embassy. I fail to understand what interest you have in these troublemakers and I question what business you have in Corocoro in the first place."

O'Neal felt his stomach knot. The holes in their plan had gone unnoticed until now. However, Morales had brought Fanelli and Murphy from their cell, which was the goal of the masquerade anyway.

Fanelli and Murphy had looked better. Both men had several bruises on their faces and necks. The cops hadn't been too gentle with them. Numerous other bruises on their torsos were concealed beneath their clothing. Both men had sobered up pretty quickly after they'd been arrested. They managed to hide their surprise when they saw O'Neal and Wentworth. Neither man said a word and both pretended they'd never seen the Hard Corps officers before.

"We explain everything, Lieutenant," Wentworth began, approaching the policemen. "You see, we were in Corocoro because Mr. Durkan has an unfortunate reputation for getting into trouble—"

"Durkan?" Morales frowned. "Neither of these men are named Durkan. We have their passports and visas. What is this nonsense?"

"We have proof for you, Lieutenant," O'Neal said as he opened the valise. "Proof that will convince you that it is important that you release these prisoners immediately."

"¡Que!" Morales glared at him. "They assaulted a police officer and resisted arrest! These *cabrones* go nowhere except back to jail. And I demand to see your identification."

"Will this do?" O'Neal inquired as he removed a hand grenade from the briefcase and pulled out the pin.

"¡Madre de Dios!" Morales gasped.

Fanelli quickly pulled the door shut before anyone in the corridor could see what had happened. The cops were unarmed and stood motionless, stunned by the unexpected threat. O'Neal shoved the briefcase along the table to Wentworth. The Hard Corps XO reached inside and drew a Browning pistol from the valise.

"Everybody stay calm and nobody gets hurt," O'Neal

announced. "Anybody gives us any trouble and we all get blown to hell together. *¿Comprende?*"

"I looked inside that briefcase," Veaga said in a dazed voice. "How . . . ?"

"Figure it out later," O'Neal snapped. "Take the cuffs off those men and keep your mouth shut."

"You will not get away with this," Morales warned.

"That's not your concern," Wentworth told him. "Right now, all you have to worry about is staying alive."

Veaga unlocked Fanelli's handcuffs. Murphy impatiently waited to have his cuffs removed. The uniformed cop glanced at O'Neal, trying to decide if he could jump the merc and grab the grenade before O'Neal could release it. O'Neal smiled and nodded at him in a mute challenge. The cop decided to abandon the notion.

Wentworth removed a coil of nylon rope from the briefcase while Vega unlocked Murphy's handcuffs. The Irishman suddenly shoved Morales into the wall and rammed a knee into the cop's gut. He slugged Morales with both fists before Fanelli pulled him away. Murphy managed to kick the police lieutenant in the ribs as Fanelli dragged him across the room.

"That bastard worked me over with a baton wrapped in a towel so it wouldn't leave as many marks!" Murphy declared.

"I know," Fanelli growled. "I got the same treatment. This ain't a good time to try to get even."

"Help me tie them up," Wentworth ordered.

After they had bound and gagged the three cops, the Hard Corps trio and Paddy Murphy emerged from the room. Wentworth carried the briefcase in one hand and his swagger stick under his arm. The Browning was hidden under his jacket. O'Neal's right fist was jammed in a coat pocket, still holding the grenade. Fanelli and Murphy silently followed.

They left the corridor and entered the lobby where the

desk clerk and two uniformed cops were arguing with
Garcia and Raul. Steve Caine did his best to stay away
from the others. The police were clearly frustrated with the
"*peones*" and appeared to be ready to throw them out of
the station. The three Hard Corps mercs and Paddy Murphy realized they wouldn't be able to sneak past the police
to the exit.

"*¡Alto!*" the desk sergeant exclaimed when he saw the
four men step from the hallway.

He tried to stomp on an alarm button under his desk, but
Victor Garcia suddenly leaped onto the desk and swung a
large fist into the cop's face. The sergeant sprawled back
into his chair. Garcia grabbed the sergeant's shirtfront and
hauled him across the desk. The muscular DEA agent
slammed his opponent to the floor and punched him again
to make sure he was unconscious.

Steve Caine reached under his poncho and drew a Browning pistol as he quietly moved behind the two startled
uniformed cops. Both men reached for their side arms.
Caine smacked the barrel of his weapon across the back of
the closest cop's skull. The policeman fell to all fours with
a groan.

The other cop started to pull his pistol from leather, but
Raul Metza grabbed his wrist and pinned the weapon
down. The cop cursed and swung his free hand into Raul's
face. The young Indian lost his grip and staggered away
from the policeman.

Caine slashed his pistol across the cop's face. The man
fell on his back and Caine stomped a bootheel into his
belly at approximately navel level. With a sickly gasp, the
cop sat up and grabbed for his abdomen. Caine clipped
him on the jaw with the Browning and the policeman
slumped unconscious.

The cop on his knees shook his head to try to clear it.
Wentworth stepped forward and slid his swagger stick
across the man's throat. He slipped an arm under his

opponent's armpit to secure a half-nelson with his hand at the back of the cop's head. He braced the stick against his forearm to increase pressure on the guy's throat.

Wentworth held the cop as Fanelli relieved the man of his sidearm. The tough guy from Jersey stuck the pistol in the waistband of his trousers as Wentworth pressed his thumbs into nerve centers in the helpless officer's neck. The cop sighed as if happy to pass out. Wentworth released the senseless policeman.

"Nice work," O'Neal commented as he returned the pin to his hand grenade. "Now, let's get the fuck outta here."

CHAPTER 13

"I'M SORRY ABOUT what happened, Captain," Joe Fanelli told William O'Neal as the four Hard Corps mercs and Paddy Murphy sat in the back of the ancient Chevy pickup.

"Shut up," O'Neal replied gruffly. "And that goes for you too, Murphy. I figure you encouraged Joe to fall off the wagon. It won't take much to convince me to put a bullet through your thick Irish skull and toss you out on the road right now."

"I won't say a word, sir," Murphy assured him. The gunrunner realized his popularity, which hadn't been too great to start with, had reached an all-time low. O'Neal might just be pissed off enough to carry out his threat if Murphy provoked him.

The ancient three-quarter-ton Chevy bounced from one rough spot to another on the washboard dirt road that wound its way toward the eastern crest of the Cordillera Real. Victor Garcia drove the truck while Raul gave instructions. As the pickup approached the Upper Yungas, the sun rose into the morning sky.

"I know I'm still on everybody's shit list," Fanelli began. "But I wonder if somebody'd be good enough to tell me where the hell we're going?"

"We're going to Raul's village," O'Neal answered.

"We made a deal with him after he told us you and Murphy were in jail. He helped us break you out of the joint and we're going to help his village fight off a bunch of bandits who've been preying on his people for about a year. Apparently, the bastards are connected with El Dorado. They abduct Indians for slave labor—like the guys we set free at the *coquito* base. The bandits have also been ripping off Indians who have coca leaves for personal use."

"Raul's village has its own stash, huh?" Fanelli remarked.

"The Indians don't use the coca leaves to make cocaine," Steve Caine commented as he squatted on the bed of the truck. "Traditionally, they chew the coca leaves like chewing gum or tobacco. They get an effect similar to a cup of coffee or a cigarette. A very mild stimulant. Some South Americans also use coca leaves for tribal ceremonies, the way Indians in the U.S. used to use peyote and magic mushrooms for rituals."

"And then some assholes in the twentieth century decided to make a profit by encouraging people to have rituals every night with little white powder up the nose," Fanelli mused.

"Until the turn of the century," Wentworth added, "cocaine wasn't even regarded as a dangerous substance. Then it was figured out that coke was one of the most addictive drugs known to man. Physically, mentally, and any other way you care to look at it. Even when it was still legal, people were committing crimes to support the habit."

"Jesus, you'd think people would have learned not to mess with that crap by now," Fanelli remarked.

"Yeah," O'Neal added. "Just like you would have thought a guy who's known he's an alcoholic for ten years would have known better than to start drinking in the middle of a mission."

"Oh, shit," Fanelli groaned.

"Listen up, Joe," O'Neal said sharply. "This unit is

not, never has been, and never will be a goddamn Ranger team. I don't expect to have to ride herd on any member of the unit. And I don't intend to. You know damn good and well you can't handle booze. That's especially true at these altitudes. You put our mission at risk as well as the lives of everybody in the unit.''

"Would it help if I reminded the captain that alcoholism is considered a disease by the AMA?'' Fanelli said hopefully.

"You're saying you're too sick to do your duty?'' O'Neal asked.

"No,'' Fanelli replied with a shrug. "Just lookin' for a cop-out that might save my ass from being bitten in half.''

"I don't give a damn what the AMA says,'' O'Neal continued. "If you want to be part of this unit, you'll keep away from booze at least for the rest of this mission.''

"I thought the bloody mission was over,'' Murphy remarked.

"Think again,'' O'Neal snapped. "We bailed you out last night, Murphy. That means you're with us for this little job in Raul's village. If you get in any more trouble, I won't be inclined to pull your nuts out of the fire again. Might even enjoy watching them roast. You understand what I mean?''

"I understand,'' Murphy said glumly.

"Captain?'' Fanelli began. "Does anybody have any idea what the odds are going to be like? I mean, how many bandits are we gonna be up against and how well armed are they?''

"Raul figures there are about fifty of them and they're well armed,'' O'Neal answered. "Apparently they've got automatic weapons.''

"In case you don't remember,'' Murphy said dryly, "we *don't* have any automatic weapons since we ditched the Uzis and M-16s.''

"I seem to recall that,'' O'Neal answered. "You're a gunrunner. Where can we get some decent firepower?''

"Out here?" the Irishman glared at him. "You've got to be jokin', Captain. Make yourselves some slingshots and I hope you're good with them, because you'll find nothing but rocks out here."

"It's a start," Caine said with a shrug.

"Your Katu training has come in very useful, Steve," Wentworth told him. "But we'll need more than spears and arrows to deal with fifty opponents armed with machine guns."

"We'll figure out strategy after we get to the village," O'Neal announced.

The village was located in the Middle Yungas, the true semitropical heads of the mountain valleys to the east of the Cordillera Real. It was a small hamlet, consisting of a handful of shacklike houses surrounded by the crop fields of the farming community. Strands of low-hanging clouds drifted above the village, creating a dreamlike atmosphere of peace and tranquility.

The Chevy pickup rolled into the village like a mechanical invader that had slipped backward into a portion of time where it didn't belong. Figures dressed in peasant garments darted behind houses, fearful of the newcomers. Garcia stepped on the brake and the truck came to a halt.

"Raul," O'Neal called softly to the youth in the front seat, "what's proper behavior for outsiders when visiting for the first time? We don't want to make a bad impression on your people five minutes after we arrive."

"Wait here," Raul urged. "It is all right if you get out of the truck, but stand by the vehicle and wait quietly. It is polite to wait for the *jilacata*, the village elder or chief, to approach, and allow him to speak first."

The Hard Corps, Murphy, Garcia, and Raul climbed from the pickup and waited as instructed. Three minutes passed before a wrinkled old man shuffled forward with the assistance of a knotty wood stave. The *jilacata* spoke with Raul in the Aymara language. The Hard Corps mercs and Paddy Murphy had no idea what the Indians were saying. Garcia listened carefully and occasionally nodded his head. The mercenaries hoped this was as positive as it appeared to be.

"I have explained to the *jilacata* why I have brought you here," Raul told them. "He bids you welcome to our village."

"That's nice," O'Neal said, nodding at the old man. The chief's leathery brown features seemed frozen in a solemn expression. "I can see he's really thrilled about this."

"My people are distrustful of strangers," Raul apologized.

"All people are distrustful of strangers," Wentworth commented. "That's part of our inherited survival nature."

"You planning to do a special for *National Geographic*?" Fanelli muttered sourly.

"I will take you to my uncle's house," Raul continued. "It has remained empty since he was murdered by Weisal and his band of El Dorado pigs."

"Wait a minute," O'Neal began. "Weisal? You mean Adolf Weisal, the Nazi war criminal?"

"What?" Garcia asked with surprise. "A Nazi war criminal connected with the *coquitos*?"

"I don't know any more about that than you do," O'Neal answered. "But I've seen a file on Weisal. The Israeli Mossad intelligence outfit has been looking for him since World War II. They figured Weisal had fled to South America. Not surprising since Eichmann, Mengele, and Barbie wound up in this part of the world. Can't say as I remember what Weisal was alleged to have done, but the Israelis must have a pretty serious grudge toward the old fart."

"Weisal is not an old man," Raul corrected. "I have seen him more than once. He is tall, perhaps taller than you. His eyes are also blue, like yours, Captain. But his manner is very different. Weisal is arrogant, disrespectful of our people, and callous to our plight. He doesn't seem to find any pleasure in what he does to us, but it clearly doesn't bother him either. He is . . . I'm not sure of the word in English.''

''Indifferent?'' Wentworth suggested.

''I suppose he is different,'' Raul said, unsure what Wentworth meant.

''He sounds like a goddamn prick to me,'' Fanelli said. ''Maybe it's like father, like son.''

''Could be,'' O'Neal agreed. ''If Adolf Weisal supervised his kid's education, he'd probably try to make a junior clone of himself. I almost hope that's what happened. Ever since my dad told me about World War II, I've always wanted to kill a Nazi.''

''Touching,'' Caine said in a monotone, which disguised the intent of the remark.

''I'll take you to my uncle's house,'' Raul invited. ''Please, follow me.''

He escorted the group through the village to a fiber suspension bridge that spanned a steep gorge. Fanelli whispered softly as he stared down at the frothy cataract of white water that cascaded down the gorge. He guessed the drop would be at least three hundred feet.

''I wonder how old this bridge is,'' Wentworth remarked. ''Incredible how something this primitive and crudely built can survive for decades.''

''Some of the wood is starting to rot,'' Caine stated as he stepped calmly from plank to plank. ''And a couple of ropes look a little frayed.''

''Will you two change the subject?'' Murphy pleaded as he shuffled nervously across the bridge.

Raul's uncle had been an introvert who lived beyond the village at the other side of the bridge. His shack wasn't big enough for more than three adult males to even find room on the floor to sleep inside. O'Neal peered across the bridge and saw numerous villagers were watching them. The timid Indians had emerged from their homes now that the strangers were safely outside their community. The elder spoke with his people.

O'Neal noticed the Indians appeared scrawny and under-fed. The crops hadn't done well that year or, just as likely, El Dorado had decided to help themselves to the lion's share of the food. Men and women glanced fearfully at the mercenaries. Most of the children stared at the newcomers with undisguised fascination.

"If we're gonna organize these people to fight," O'Neal remarked to Garcia, "we'll have to convince them to trust us."

"That might not be so easy," the DEA agent replied. "The Aymara aren't real big on trust. Can't blame them really. The Aymara once belonged to a sophisticated civilization, until the conquistadores came in and destroyed the Aymaran political and cultural systems. At the same time, the Indians had no intention of assimilating into the society the Spanish wanted. So the Indians in Bolivia have become strangers in their own nation. This is a real problem for the central government. About half of the population are pure Indians. Many of these have simply refused to learn Spanish because they're still pissed off at the Europeans for past treatment. They don't want to get involved with outsiders. Most strangers have screwed around with the Indians and tried to shove American or European notions down their throats."

"Wonderful," O'Neal replied. "Let's take a look around. I want to see what we're supposed to do here."

"Thought that was obvious," Garcia replied. "We're supposed to protect the village."

"Setting up defenses might not be so easy. If we can't get any automatic weapons or something to even out the odds a little, we're gonna be sunk before the bandits show up," O'Neal stated. "If we try to take them on while we're only armed with a few pistols, we might as well spare the bastards time and simply kill ourselves . . . or run.''

"Suicide is out of the question," Garcia said with a shrug. "I'm Catholic. I'll steal cars and trucks, shoot guys in the back, and beat the shit out of cops, but I draw the line at suicide. I'm not worried about a little Purgatory, but risking eternal damnation is another matter.''

"None of us will sacrifice our lives in a vain gesture of defiance," O'Neal assured him. He peered out at the steep mountainside, considering how much gravity would be on their side.

The area was a great location for a village. Forests of hardwoods were only a few miles away. The source of flowing water was ideal for irrigation and could have been used to power turbogenerators such as the machines used at the Hard Corps compound. Indeed, the green oasis might have been used as a health resort during the Incan empire.

"The road, if one can call it that, doesn't branch or loop," Wentworth remarked as he approached O'Neal. "There's one way in and one way out, if our opponents use cars or trucks. If they've got enough guts they might be able to storm uphill on the ground on motorcycles or horseback. My guess is they'll go on foot.''

"We might be able to let a few through and cut off the rest," Caine suggested. "A tank trap at the entrance could block off the enemy vehicles.''

"My people will start digging immediately," Raul announced enthusiastically.

"Not just yet, amigo," O'Neal urged. "We've got two big problems to deal with first. We don't have enough weapons to fight the bandits, and from the looks of your people, they aren't ready to back us up.''

"They're afraid to even look at us," Wentworth added, watching the villagers turn their heads to avoid facing the mercs. "I'm afraid I can't be very confident in their willingness to fight even if we can get weapons for them."

"But you will teach them, *sí*?" Raul asked hopefully.

"Teach them to fight with machetes and hoes against submachine guns?" O'Neal shook his head. "Sorry, Raul. If we can't get our hands on some decent firepower . . ."

"You need guns, señor," a voice announced from the shack which had formerly belonged to Raul's uncle. "I know where you can find them."

"The old one!" Raul exclaimed with surprise.

The Hard Corps half-expected to see the *jilacata* emerge from the shack, although they couldn't figure out how the village elder could have gotten across the bridge and hidden in the house without supernatural assistance. However, a different old man emerged from the building. The ancient Indian appeared to be even older than the *jilacata*. His chestnut-brown skin resembled wrinkled parchment and white hair hung from his head in long strands. Yet, he walked without the assistance of a cane, and a wiry smile split his deeply creased face.

"This is the old one," Raul explained as if the title was the name of a world-famous celebrity. "He is a Collahuaya healer. A man of medicine and mysticism. The wisest man you will ever meet in Bolivia. Possibly the world."

"The boy exaggerates," the old man said with a grin. "Not much, but he still exaggerates. So you are the men we have been waiting for."

"You knew we were coming?" O'Neal frowned, unable to see how this was possible.

"In my fashion," the old one replied with a nod. "I sent Raul to La Paz to meet with an American Drug Enforcement agent named Rodriguez."

"I knew Rodriguez," Victor Garcia remarked, grimly. "He was murdered by El Dorado."

"He was a very brave man," Raul declared. "Señor Rodriguez died fighting. He killed two *coquitos* before the bastards shot him in the back."

"Yes," the old man agreed. "Yet, before Raul and I parted company that day, we had discussed the possibility that Señor Rodriguez might not be able to help us. We agreed that, if this proved true, we would have to find someone else. Hungry warriors who, for whatever reason, would help us fight Weisal and his El Dorado slavers. I know Raul well enough to know he would not return to the village until he had found the men that we needed."

"You guessed right," O'Neal replied. "Circumstances sort of put us in a ripe position to be recruited for the job."

"Fate," the old one said with a smile.

"Damned if I know," the Hard Corps commander said with a shrug. "Raul took a big risk. We might have just gone along with him until we'd escaped from Corocoro and either dumped him on the road or killed him."

"But you didn't," the old man stated. "Fate has brought us honorable men. The best warriors have always been such men."

"That might be true in the tales of King Arthur and the Knights of the Round Table," Wentworth commented. "But in reality, men without honor can win battles too. Especially if they're better armed."

"I told you I know where you can get guns," the ancient Collahuaya healer declared. "Providing my information is correct."

"Well, so far your information has been right on the money," O'Neal remarked. "I sure hope that trend continues."

CHAPTER 14

THE GUNS THAT the old one spoke of were an alleged cache of arms buried by the guerrilla soldiers of Che Guevara during the Cuban rebel's unsuccessful efforts to coordinate a peasant-based revolution in Bolivia. Guevara's revolution plans ended on October 9, 1967, when the Bolivian army captured the guerrilla leader and executed him near Vallegrande.

The old man led Wentworth, Fanelli, and Murphy to the site at the outskirts of Potosí. The burial site was supposed to be covered by a mound of rocks located between two small knolls half a kilometer west of the railroad tracks. The four men eventually found the site and began clearing away rocks and smaller rubble.

"It's a good thing they didn't pick living or active geographical features of the land to mark the site," James Wentworth remarked as he hauled away several stones with his hands. "Trees or streambeds could change a lot in twenty years. We could be digging around here for years."

"I just hope there's something buried here," Murphy complained. "I've been runnin' guns in Bolivia for nearly eight years now and I never heard about Che having any secret caches of weapons."

"The man who told me about the guns was a former

guerrilla in Che's private army," the old man explained, repeating his story for the third or fourth time. "He has been living in Machacamarca under a different identity ever since Che was killed. Needless to say, he did not want the authorities to know he used to be a Communist rebel. He is still fearful of retribution. However, I knew his father and I was aware that he had been one of Guevara's followers. When I asked him to help my village fight the *coquitos*, he told me of the weapons cache after I gave my word I would not reveal the truth about his past."

"Bloody Red bastard probably lied through his teeth," Murphy murmured, lifting a skull-size rock from the mound. "Say, do they have any nice quiet *cantinas* in Potosí?"

"This isn't a goddamn pass to go into town and—" Fanelli began. He stopped in mid-sentence when his fingers probed under a layer of dirt at the last of the rocks. "Hey, I feel something. There's something buried here."

"Let's not take all day," Wentworth urged as he began scooping up handfuls of dirt and clearing it from the site. They soon uncovered the top of a broad plastic tarpaulin. Fanelli drew a knife from its sheath and slit the plastic down the center. He peeled back the tarp and the men peered inside. The pungent smell of packing grease met their nostrils as they stared at the metal objects below.

"Well, I'll be the illegitimate son of a London gutter slut," Murphy whispered in astonishment.

They hauled out the weapons. The arms were an assortment of Communist-manufactured firearms from the 1960s. The two Hard Corps mercs had good reason to recognize the weapons because the NVA and the Vietcong had used the same type of guns in Vietnam.

They tallied up the weapons. There were five Soviet-made AK-47 assault rifles and a Chinese Type-50 submachine gun with several crates of 7.62-mm ammunition. Fanelli picked up one of two MAT-49 submachine guns among the collection.

"This sucker brings back memories," he remarked. "They used these French choppers in 'Nam. Had a bunch of 'em left over from when the French occupied Indo-China. The Commies altered the MAT-49s to fire 7.62 instead of nine-mill ammo. Both of these babies have been converted. Bet these guns would have wound up in 'Nam if Che's boys hadn't gotten a hold of 'em."

"Yeah," Wentworth agreed as he raised a long bazooka-like weapon. "But this is the crown jewel of the entire collection. A Soviet RPG-7 rocket launcher with five rounds of explosive warheads."

"I'm glad you fellas are so thrilled about this," Murphy complained, "because all we've got are nine additional weapons. You really think that's going to be enough to make a difference?"

"Well," Wentworth replied with a shrug, "I guess it'll have to do. Won't it?"

"Saints preserve us," the Irishman moaned. "We're all going to die."

A young boy ran to the house that had formerly belonged to Raul's uncle. The youngster called out to the men inside the building. William O'Neal, Victor Garcia, and Raul Metza emerged from the house as the boy delivered a rapid message in his native tongue.

"Two trucks are coming up the main road," Raul translated. "The *jilacata* thinks they are El Dorado."

"Find Steve," O'Neal told Raul. "He should be by the west end of the village. Tell him what's happened and warn him not to jump to conclusions. We have to wait to make certain of what we're up against before we take action."

"*Sí,* señor," Raul replied as he dashed in the direction where Caine had last been seen.

O'Neal and Garcia headed to the center of the village. The Indians remained out of sight, fearful of the possible bloodshed that might erupt at any second. O'Neal moved to the cover of a tree trunk and watched the vehicles approach. The trucks were four-wheel-drive pickups, one trailing cautiously behind the other. Two men were stationed in the backs of the trucks, armed with Uzi submachine guns.

"They're not military personnel," O'Neal announced when he noticed none of the men in the vehicles wore uniforms. "And I don't think they're cops."

"El Dorado," Garcia rasped, reaching under his poncho for a Browning pistol. "No doubt about it."

The enemy vehicles came to an abrupt halt. The *coquitos* sensed danger or suspected something about the village wasn't quite right. O'Neal cursed under his breath as he realized what was wrong. The village was too quiet. The Indians were hiding from view.

"They're not within pistol range," Garcia commented.

"Wait," was all O'Neal could suggest. "It's their move."

Suddenly, the battered Chevy pickup appeared on the road a few hundred yards behind the hoodlums' vehicles. Fanelli peered through the windshield at the trucks blocking the road ahead. He stomped on the brakes when he saw enemy gunmen turn their Uzi toward the Chevy.

"Holy fuck!" Murphy exclaimed as he ducked behind the dashboard.

Wentworth rose from the back of the Chevy, the Russian RPG-7 in his fists. The Hard Corps XO promptly triggered the rocket launcher. The launching charge puffed white smoke and the cone-shaped grenade head leaped forward. The rocket motor ignited and the antitank-shaped charge hurled into the nearest *coquito* pickup.

The explosion blasted the truck to bits. Twisted metal and charred bodies hurtled into the air. Flaming gasoline splashed the second El Dorado rig. An enemy gunman jumped from the back of the pickup to avoid the fiery liquid. The driver stomped on the accelerator, eager to put some distance between himself and the men in the Chevy truck.

Paddy Murphy emerged from the passenger side of the Chevy as Fanelli stepped from the driver's side. The Hard Corps merc grabbed a MAT-49 from the floorboards while his Irish companion seized an AK-47 assault rifle.

The Uzi-wielding killer who'd bailed out of the enemy rig swung his weapon toward the Chevy. Fanelli and Murphy opened fire. Twin streams of 7.62-mm slugs chewed through the gunman's chest. His body hopped and wiggled backward several feet before it fell lifeless to the ground.

The *coquito* truck rolled forward toward the village. O'Neal and Garcia held their Browning pistols in firm, double-hand grips and opened fire. Four 9-mm rounds struck the pickup's windshield. The driver cried out and slumped behind the wheel, throwing the truck off course. The rig slid off the road and two tires plunged into a long pit. Sharp wooden punji sticks in the bed of the pit punctured rubber and the truck came to a full stop.

''*¡Cochinos!*'' a furious and frightened El Dorado hitman screamed as he pushed open the passenger door and emerged with an Ingram MAC-10 in his fists.

Steve Caine had notched an arrow to the bowstring of his favorite long-range silent weapon. The Hard Corps merc raised the bow and pulled back the arrow as he aimed with care. Caine released the feathered butt of the arrow and let the missile fly.

The razor-sharp Alaskan broadhead hit the gunman in the right side of the lower back. As it passed clean through his body, the arrow severed the kidney from the adrenal gland, causing massive shock to his system. The bandit's legs collapsed beneath him. His body twitched wildly for a moment or two and ceased moving forever.

''That was an incredible shot, señor,'' Raul Metza said with astonishment as he stood next to Steve Caine. The Indian youth guessed that the arrow had traveled at least twenty meters before it nailed the *coquito* target.

"Not really," Caine sighed as he lowered his bow. "I only wanted to wound him so we could question the son of a bitch."

The villagers ventured timidly from their homes and stared in astonishment at the burning wreckage of one El Dorado truck and the disabled remains of the other. Suddenly, several Indians began to cheer as they realized their mysterious guests had defeated the El Dorado scouts.

"Sounds like somebody liked the show," Wentworth commented as the Chevy pulled up in front of O'Neal and Garcia.

"I just hope they decide to participate in the future," the Hard Corps commander replied. "You guys showed up just in time."

"So we have a flair for the melodramatic," Wentworth answered. "Want to see what we obtained while we were out shopping?"

The old man rose slowly from the back of the truck. He smiled at O'Neal as he handed the Hard Corps leader an AK-47. O'Neal examined the weapon with appreciation and nodded.

"Very nice," he confirmed. "Your story about Che's cache was true. How many of these do we have?"

"Five Kalashnikov rifles, three submachine guns, some crates of 7.62-mm ammo, and the rocket launcher," Fanelli answered as he climbed out of the Chevy. "A couple of the enemy weapons might work, too."

"Ten or eleven guns." O'Neal frowned. "We'll need more than that."

"Maybe we can come up with something else," Fanelli mused. "Do any of these farmers have any ammonium nitrate?"

"Don't get fancy, Joe," Wentworth snorted. "Ammonium nitrate is found in many commercial fertilizers, right?"

"Well, that's how I figured I'd probably get my hands on some," Fanelli admitted.

"My people generally use bat guano," the old man answered. "They get it from traders from Peru. They have been doing this for almost a thousand years."

"Can you make bat shit explode, Joe?" O'Neal wanted to know.

"If it's humanly possible," Fanelli answered, "I can do it."

"Then you'd better get to working on the project," O'Neal declared. "And the rest of us had best concentrate on training these Indians so maybe they can help us fight. Steve probably has some other dirty tricks in mind. His punji-stick booby trap worked well enough."

"Yeah," Garcia agreed. "The instant the tires hit those stakes, the truck was out of the game. You fellas learn that trick in 'Nam?"

"We're gonna need every trick we can come up with," O'Neal stated grimly. "The enemy sent this scout detail to check on the village. That means El Dorado is probably planning to make a visit pretty soon, and when the scouts don't return, Weisal or whoever's in charge will be back here in much larger numbers. The next fight won't be so easy."

CHAPTER 15

THE HARD CORPS spent the next three days preparing the village to defend itself when the *coquitos* returned. Since they only had a handful of weapons and limited ammunition, the mercs couldn't give the Indians proper instruction in the use of firearms. They taught the fundamentals to a few of the villagers, but circumstances prevented them from really teaching the Indians enough for them to develop any real skill. The Hard Corps, Garcia, and Murphy would have to do most of the shooting.

A variety of booby traps and improvised weapons was manufactured. Caine taught basic archery skills to some of the more promising students. It seemed ironic that a white guy from a middle-class family in Michigan was teaching Indians how to use a bow and arrow, but the Aymara had never been an aggressive people. They were farmers and traders, not warriors or accomplished hunters.

Wentworth instructed some of the Indians in stick fighting. They learned to look at hoes and shovels as improvised weapons as well as tools. They were taught some fine points in knife fighting and how to wield a machete with defensive and offensive cuts and thrusts. The villagers were amazed to discover that everyday tools could be lethal weapons. The Hard Corps were equally astonished that the Aymara seemed so totally ignorant of anything concerning fighting and self-defense. Yet, the Indians' culture had long been one of cooperation and constructive unity. Aggression had always been discouraged because it got in the way of the productive desires of the farming community. This served to make the Aymara a very peaceful and harmonious society, but it also made them helpless targets for others who chose to prey on them.

Until now.

The Hard Corps realized that there was a limit to what they could hope to accomplish in a short period of time. Transforming a basically pacifistic village into an effective fighting unit wasn't easy. El Dorado, however, was accustomed to violence. The *coquitos* wouldn't hesitate to kill and they were better armed than the Indian villagers.

"If I was to make a wager on who'd win if our side tangles with El Dorado," Paddy Murphy muttered as he knelt by a campfire next to O'Neal and Wentworth, "I think I'd be placin' my bet on the other side."

"We won't have to fight El Dorado," Wentworth reminded him. "We're only concerned with the splinter group led by Weisal."

"Just fifty or sixty opponents armed with machine guns?" the gunrunner snorted. "Sorry if'n that doesn't give me any reassurance. Maybe we could take the truck and make a break for it. If we drove all night and most of the following day, we could reach the border and slip into Peru."

"Maybe we'll do that after our work here is finished," O'Neal replied. "Right now we've got a contract with these people."

"Thought you blokes were mercenaries," Murphy remarked. "The villagers won't be paying us enough to make the risk worthwhile. We'll probably all get killed anyway, but it would be nice if we could look forward to some sort of reward if we survive."

"If you want to take off, Murphy," O'Neal began as he slipped an arm through the shoulder strap of an Uzi submachine gun confiscated from a dead *coquito*, "go ahead, but you're not taking the truck or any of the rifles."

"Sort of figured you'd say something like that," Murphy said with a sigh. "Damned if I can figure you fellas out."

"Don't worry about it," Wentworth told him. The Hard Corps XO glanced up at the stars in the night sky overhead. "You know, for the rainy season it sure has been dry and I don't see a cloud in the sky tonight."

"Yeah," O'Neal agreed. "We're gonna have to get Garcia to contact the CIA again and find out if they can get us out of the country now."

"Maybe they don't want to get us out," Wentworth suggested grimly. "Could be the Company plans to leave us stranded and hope we get killed so they won't have to worry about us being an embarrassment."

"Well," O'Neal said with a shrug, "we're expendable, but then so is everybody else. CIA would probably like to get us out of Bolivia because even dead we'll be a problem for them. People will still figure out who sent us and the Company will be under fire for meddling in foreign affairs. If we're gone, the official story will be cocaine syndicate goons killing each other. Nobody is gonna get too excited about that."

"Jesus!" Murphy exclaimed as he saw a pair of legs appear suddenly beside him. The Irishman hadn't heard anyone approach. The figure had seemed to materialize from thin air.

"Sorry," Caine said without much concern for the fact he'd startled the gunrunner.

"What's up?" O'Neal asked, climbing to his feet.

"Company coming," Caine answered, jerking his head toward the road. "Four vehicles are approaching. A couple of them have searchlights mounted to the rigs."

"Sounds like El Dorado is back," O'Neal declared. "Get the others ready. Looks like this time could be for real."

A Jeep and three pickup trucks drove along the stringer road toward the center of the village. The wreckage of the two El Dorado trucks that had arrived earlier had been dragged away and all signs of the carnage had been removed. Powerful searchlights threw bright beams across the village as the vehicles drew closer.

The Jeep came to a halt as the pickups moved around it to form a horseshoe around the village. Headlights and searchlights filled the community with a bright glare. There was little movement within the village. A few Indians stood by open doors. Two figures sat on the ground, backs braced against the wall of a house. Alpaca ponchos covered their bodies and the brims of their hats were tilted over their faces.

"The *indios* are lazy tonight," Ramon Delgadillo remarked as he stood at the back of the Jeep with his arms folded along a crossbar. "Jose! Esteban! Go wake up those two toads."

Delgadillo was Erik Weisal's second-in-command. When the heavyset cholo barked orders, the *coquitos* jumped. Two El Dorado thugs rushed forward as Delgadilla stepped slowly from his vehicle and drew an old cavalry saber from a scabbard on his hip. He brandished the weapon in an exaggerated manner in an attempt to frighten the Aymara Indians.

"We need some new recruits to help with business," he announced. "Besides, some of my men would like a woman or two for some recreation tonight."

The two flunkies approached the figures that appeared to be napping by the wall. One *coquito* carried an American-made M-16 rifle. He leaned forward and poked the barrel into the ribs of one of the seated men.

The poncho flapped back and Victor Garcia's hands grabbed the gunman's rifle. The muscular DEA agent pulled hard and yanked the startled *coquito* off-balance to plunge headfirst into the wall. Garcia held on to the gun barrel and shoved hard. The hard plastic stock hit the *coquito* under the jaw and he toppled unconscious to the ground.

The second El Dorado goon turned toward the ruckus. His attention moved from the other ''sleeping'' figure. William O'Neal rose to his feet suddenly and pushed aside his poncho to reveal a Browning pistol in his fist. His arm swung a fast cross-body stroke and chopped the butt of the Browning into the side of the gunman's neck. The thug groaned and wilted to the ground.

Ramon Delgadillo quickly thrust his sword, point first, into the ground and unslung an Ingram MAC-10 from his shoulder. Garcia dashed suddenly around the corner of the house while William O'Neal dove for cover behind a thick tree trunk. Delgadillo and several of his henchmen opened fire. The air was alive with high-velocity bullets as automatic weapons snarled in unison.

One attacker dropped his gun suddenly and grabbed at his neck, trying to pull the two-foot-long shaft of an arrow from his throat. The man fell to his knees, but none of his comrades noticed he was dying. He wasn't the only one.

James Wentworth aimed an AK-47 around the corner of a house. The merc adopted a kneeling stance and used the building to brace the barrel of his weapon as he peered through the sights of the Kalashnikov. The front sight found the head of an enemy *coquito*. He squeezed the trigger. A 7.62-mm round drilled into the man's skull directly through his ear, enlarging the natural opening and leaving a bloody, gaping cavity when it exited at the opposite side.

Steve Caine launched another arrow from his camouflaged position among the branches of a tall maguroy tree. The missile struck another *coquito* in the chest, left of center. The steel tip burrowed into the man's heart. Two

other archers fired arrows into the invading forces. Their
crudely made bows lacked the power and accuracy of
Caine's weapon, but one arrow found human flesh. An El
Dorado killer doubled up in agony with the wooden shaft
of an arrow jutting from his stomach.

Delgadillo hadn't lost confidence in the firepower of his
men, but he simply didn't see any targets to shoot at. The
village defenders were well concealed and they'd managed
to take out half a dozen of Delgadillo's men. He abandoned his saber and ducked behind the Jeep as a salvo of
automatic fire tore into the ground near his feet.

William O'Neal had grabbed his Uzi behind the tree. He
leaned around the edge of the trunk and triggered the
weapon. A burst of 9-mm rounds raked the torsos of two
coquito gunmen who had ventured closer to the village.

Paddy Murphy fired a Kalashnikov rifle from the doorway of the adobe church. The gunrunner saw an El Dorado
goon topple to the ground with a trio of bullet holes in his
chest. Murphy aimed his weapon again, but a bullet chipped
adobe from the corner of the doorway. Murphy hissed an
obscenity and ducked behind cover.

Delgadillo climbed into the Jeep and ordered the driver
to swing around and retreat. The guy gladly obliged. The
jeep spun about and the trucks followed. All four vehicles
drove off the road in order to turn around.

"Step into my parlor," Joe Fanelli rasped as he crawled
to a car battery hidden behind some shrubs.

Fanelli had taken the battery from one of the earlier El
Dorado vehicles that had previously tangled with the Hard
Corps. He had also rigged a series of makeshift land mines
across the grounds that the enemy vehicles were driving
over. The mines dotted the landscape like a series of
half-buried stones. Fanelli waited patiently, his hands on
two wires leading to the minefield.

The four El Dorado vehicles finished their turn and
prepared to flee. One of the pickup trucks hit the punji-

stick bed. The rig shifted sideways into the pit, tires punctured by the sharp stakes. The truck limped along the trench and came to an awkward halt.

The other three vehicles moved farther into the mine-field. Fanelli touched the bare wires together to charge the homemade bombs with the battery. The "stones" ex-ploded into deadly bursts of flying metal, broken glass and red-hot fragments of chicken wire.

The multiple blasts tore into tires and shattered win-dows. One truck was virtually on top of a mine when it went off. The explosion ignited the fuel tank. The pickup burst into a flaming spray of mangled metal and burned human parts. The Jeep managed to escape more or less unscathed, but the remaining pickup truck waddled onto the road with two flat tires and a ruptured radiator.

Several *coquitos* darted about on foot, uncertain if they should run or fight. The Hard Corps left them no choice. The mercs opened fire and cut down three opponents with a hailstorm of bullets. The slain El Dorado goons twitched in the dust while survivors dashed for cover behind the disabled truck stuck in the punji pit.

An arrow chased one hoodlum as he ran for shelter. The projectile struck him in the back and pierced his spine between the shoulder blades. The man sprawled on his belly as Victor Garcia rushed forward and fired a con-verted MAT-49 submachine gun. Bullets ripped through the rib cage of another *coquito* gunman. The thug's blood-ied body hurtled forward and crashed into the frame of the pickup before slumping lifeless to the ground.

Raul Metza circled around the road, a bottle in his fist. The Indian youth had filled the bottle with kerosene and stuck a cloth in the mouth of the bottle. He crept closer to the enemy position and struck a match to ignite the cloth fuse of the Molotov cocktail. He reared up and hurled the bottle at the pickup.

The bottle missed its mark by a few yards. Flaming

liquid splashed the *coquitos* behind the truck. Screaming figures bolted into view, their clothes and hair covered with crackling fire.

The victims staggered across the road as O'Neal and Garcia opened fire. Bullets slammed into the burning hoodlums and put them out of their misery forever. One *coquito* threw himself to the ground and rolled in the dirt to extinguish the flames, his prone body sprawled beneath the wave of bullets that slashed air above his rolling form.

The burned man rose to one knee and drew a revolver from his belt. James Wentworth promptly shot him in the face with a trio of AK-47 rounds. The man's body fell backward, blood flowing from the stump of its neck and the messy glob of skull fragments and loose skin that had formerly been a head.

"Hold your fire!" O'Neal shouted. "They're finished!"

The Indians cheered the second victory against the *coquitos*, but the Hard Corps didn't waste time patting themselves on the back. The mercs checked the enemy to make certain none of them were playing 'possum. Steve Caine hurried to the two dazed El Dorado thugs who'd been knocked unconscious at the beginning of the battle. He relieved the prisoners of weapons and kept them covered with a Chicom T-50 submachine gun.

Fanelli and Garcia checked inside the disabled pickup while O'Neal, Wentworth, and Murphy gathered up weapons and ammo from slain opponents. Raul moved forward to assist.

"Nice work with the Molotov, Raul," O'Neal told him. "You saved us a lot of time and maybe a life or two in the process."

"Thank you," Raul said with a nervous smile. "I . . . I was terrified and I . . . I think I may be ill."

"We were all scared," O'Neal assured him. "And you always feel a little sick after a battle. The first time is always the hardest. Don't be ashamed of it. All part of being human.''

"Well," Murphy began with a cheerful laugh, "I imagine El Dorado will be off licking their wounds for a while after this.''

"They won't have time," O'Neal declared. "We're going after them. Gather up the gear and let's head back to the truck. *Our* truck, that is. We still have more work to do tonight.''

"Are you certain this is a good time for an offensive?'' Garcia asked, a trace of doubt in his voice.

"*Any* time is a good time for an offensive,'' the Hard Corps commander replied with a positive nod.

CHAPTER 16

ERIK WEISAL sat at the field desk inside the tent set up for his command center while the *coquitos* conducted operations in the Yungas. Ramon Delgadillo stood rigidly in front of Weisal's desk. He had just finished explaining why he had returned from the Aymara village without any hostages because most of his men had been slaughtered in a fierce battle with the villagers.

"Donnerwetter dochmal!" Weisal cursed, slipping into German in his rage. He slammed his fist on the desk top. "Those damned *indios* have never put up any sort of organized armed resistance before."

"Someone was helping them, jefe," Delgadillo said lamely. "I thought I heard voices shout something in English during the fight. The Indians must have gotten some norteamericanos to help defend the village."

"Norteamericanos?" Weisal sneered. "You're telling me that your people couldn't deal with a handful of yanqui scum from the United States? My father told me about them. They're a nation of weaklings, corrupted by gutless politicians and Jews."

"Did your father also tell you that after the United States got involved in World War II," Delgadillo replied, "the Nazis started to lose the war?"

Weisal glared at his second-in-command, but Delgadillo met his gaze without flinching. He was a cholo, part Indian and part Spanish, so he didn't appreciate the Nazi notions of Aryan purity and power to the "Master Race." Delgadillo didn't feel like listening to Weisal spout half-baked propaganda that he'd heard from his senile old man.

"I don't mean to speak with disrespect for your father," Delgadillo lied, "but it is a dangerous mistake to underestimate the men helping the *indios* because they might be yanquis. Whoever they are, *whatever* they are, they're very good at their job. They're not only skilled fighters but good strategists and organizers as well."

"You're right, of course," Weisal was forced to agree. "I understand many Americans are of German descent. They may indeed be formidable opponents, Ramon."

"If you'd been with us during the raid, you wouldn't have any doubts about that," Delgadillo assured him. "Maybe we should leave this village be . . ."

"No!" Weisal said angrily. "They must not be allowed to drive us away or the Indians of all the villages will defy us in this manner. We can't run from them, Ramon. That would be like a wolf pack afraid to prey on sheep because a few of the rams have horns."

"A number of men have already been killed," Delgadillo reminded him. "We'll certainly lose more if we confront them again. The enemy are armed with automatic weapons and explosives."

"So are we, Ramon," Weisal declared. "Our men have had far more time to develop their ability with weapons. They've got more experience and I'm confident that our strategy and our organization are better than any that a pack of yanqui *cochinos* can come up with."

"I'm sure you're right, jefe," Delgadillo replied.

"We'll wait a few hours," Weisal decided. "That will lull the enemy into a false sense of security. They'll think we've left or even given up. Then, just before dawn we'll strike.''

The Hard Corps had little trouble locating the *coquito* base. They simply followed the two enemy vehicles that had managed to escape from the battle at the village. Although the Jeep and truck had a head start, both had been damaged and hobbled away with at least a flat tire apiece. The Hard Corps pursued the enemy on foot.

The damaged vehicles left a trail that a blind man could follow. Gouge marks from tire hubs, radiator and oil leaks, and the mechanical groans of tortured engines in the distance left no doubt that they were tracking the right rigs. Steve Caine took the point because his Katu training made him the best tracker of the mercenary team. O'Neal, Wentworth, Fanelli, and Paddy Murphy followed on foot.

"Did it occur to anyone that these bastards might radio ahead and have reinforcements meet them before they reach their headquarters?'' Murphy inquired with a harsh whisper.

"Yeah," O'Neal answered. "We're hoping that won't happen. If it does, we'll just have to deal with the situation when it happens. Jim, tell Vic to advance.''

James Wentworth raised the antenna of a walkie-talkie. They had found two sets of the two-way radios among the gear in those vehicles taken out of the game during the battle. The mercs changed the frequencies so they could communicate with each other without broadcasting their messages to any El Dorado goons who might be using walkie-talkies at the same time.

"Road Runner, this is Bushmaster, come in," Wentworth spoke into the mouthpiece of his radio.

"Read you, Bushmaster," Victor Garcia's voice replied. "How are things up ahead? Over.''

"Quiet so far," Wentworth answered. "Advance another half mile approximate. Over.''

"Read you loud and clear," the DEA agent confirmed. "Keep in touch, good buddy. Over.''

Garcia was driving the Chevy pickup, following the Hard Corps a couple of miles behind the mercs. Four villagers, including Raul Metza, were among his cargo.

"That's a big ten-four," Wentworth said, continuing the trucker jargon that Garcia had introduced into the conversation. "Watch out for the bears. Over and out."

Progress was slow but steady and, fortunately, the enemy vehicles weren't moving much faster than the Hard Corps tracking team. Eventually, the trail led them off the dirt roads and down a worn pathway into a forest of lodgepole conifers with occasional stands of oak and lots of scrub brush. The forest had sprouted up along the base of a mountain with an old abandoned mine burrowed in the face of the rock wall.

Yellow lights glowed among the trees. The lights were steady and didn't flicker, which betrayed the fact the lights were not from campfires or a natural phenomenon caused by moonlight reflected on water. As the Hard Corps drew closer, they heard the moaning of diesel-powered generators in the distance. Shapes of pickup trucks and Jeeps appeared through the trees. Tents stood beyond the row of vehicles. Yellow lightbulbs cast a bright hue across the canvas walls of the tents.

"Jackpot," O'Neal rasped as he raised his Steiner binoculars to get a better look at the base.

The men in the camp were dressed in a variety of lightweight casual clothes, most favoring Levi's or cutoffs and white or tan bush shirts. Virtually all were armed. Some carried automatic rifles or submachine guns while others only carried pistols. The weapons were all first class, of American and European manufacture. O'Neal was confident they had found the enemy base.

"Jim," O'Neal said, turning to Wentworth, "go back to the road and tell Garcia to meet you there. You're in charge of the men in the group."

"Any ideas about how you want me to use them?"

Wentworth inquired as he raised the antenna to his
walkie-talkie.

"Cover that side," O'Neal answered, gesturing toward
the west. "We'll handle this side. The mountain will block
off one possible exit and we'll just have to make certain
they don't take off in any other direction."

"No prisoners?" Wentworth asked.

"We're not letting any of them get away this time,"
O'Neal replied. "Don't know what we'd do with prisoners, but I'm not going to order anybody to commit murder.
But, if we don't kill them they'll kill us. So nobody gets
away."

Wentworth nodded and headed back for the road. The
Hard Corps XO carried the cavalry saber Delgadillo had
left behind when he'd fled the village. Wentworth was also
armed with a Kalashnikov rifle and a Browning pistol.
Fanelli watched the merc lieutenant depart. The tough guy
from Jersey sighed and shook his head.

"You ever notice how that guy always manages to find
a goddamn sword when we're on a mission?" Fanelli
muttered. "You'd think the fuckin' things grew up outa
the ground every damn place we go."

"Don't worry about it," O'Neal replied. "Wentworth
knows what he's doing. You brought along some of those
homemade explosives of yours, Joe?"

"Yeah," Fanelli confirmed. "Not a lot. I didn't want to
dig up the mines planted at the village because those
fertilizer bombs ain't all that stable."

"That's bloody wonderful," Murphy rasped, "since
we're right beside you and you're carrying a bunch of 'em
in that sack."

"Boom!" Fanelli said with a grin.

He carried a canvas bag loaded with improvised explosives, in addition to a MAT-49 submachine gun and side
arm. Fanelli had kept the French blaster because they still

had an ample supply of 7.62-mm ammunition and their 9-mm ammo was rapidly dwindling.

This fact hadn't escaped O'Neal, but the Hard Corps commander had opted to carry an Uzi because he had a lot of faith in the weapon. Many firearms experts consider the Uzi to be the best submachine gun ever made and O'Neal was inclined to agree. An Uzi can go through hell without jamming and the rate of fire is rapid enough to create massive destruction, but not too great to reduce the ability to control the weapon.

Steve Caine carried an MAT-49 for the same reasons Fanelli had chosen to stick with the 7.62-mm piece. He also had his trusted bow, arrows, survival knife, and a Browning autoloader. Murphy had selected an M-16 taken from a slain *coquito*. The Irish gunrunner had purposefully chosen a long-range weapon with a limited ammo supply to avoid close-quarters combat with the enemy. Any reason that gave Murphy an excuse to keep some distance between himself and the enemy was a good reason in Murphy's opinion.

"Okay," O'Neal began in a harsh whisper. "Everybody lock your mouths shut. We're gonna move closer to the bastards. We've got to find out as much as possible about their setup. Steve, this is the sort of thing you specialize in."

"That's a fact," Caine said with a modest shrug. "Want me to do the recon?"

"I want to see it for myself," O'Neal answered. "We'll both go, but I'll leave the risky stuff for you. You're the expert."

"True," Caine agreed. He wasn't bragging. Both men knew O'Neal's remark was accurate. "I'll go first, sir. The *coquitos* might have some booby traps set up or there might be something else that makes the situation kind of tricky. Sort of thing I can handle best on my own."

"No argument," O'Neal assured him. He realized that a

wise commander appreciates that others have individual skills greater than his own. A leader who allows his ego to get in the way of a mission is just an insecure, rank-pulling asshole.

Caine moved forward, slipping into the shadows with ease. The Katu-trained mercenary crept silently toward the enemy base. O'Neal followed, trying to emulate Caine's stealth. The Hard Corps commander was very good at moving quietly in the dark, but he couldn't match Caine's unique talent.

Steve Caine slithered among the bushes and trees without rustling a single leaf or snapping a twig. He ducked behind a dense shrub and peered through the branches. The merc had an excellent view of the enemy compound.

Six tents were set up, forming a circle around the center of the camp. A number of dark yellow "bug lights" were strung between the tents to bathe the camp in a pale glow that, in theory at least, would reduce the number of insects in the area. Several *coquitos* were clustered at the center of the camp, discussing something in Spanish. Caine wished he understood the language, but he noticed the expressions on the faces of the hoodlums. They sure didn't look happy. Caine suspected the reason for the *coquitos'* sour attitude might have something to do with the battle-scarred Jeep and pickup among the vehicles.

The stealthiest Hard Corps member crawled silently through a patch of tall grass in order to check out the rest of the camp. He took care not to disturb the grass any more than was absolutely necessary. Caine stopped when he noticed a long, slender wire inches from his head.

Caine followed the length of the wire. It extended to the base of a tree. Mounted against the trunk was a cut-down shotgun. It was a crude, makeshift weapon of iron pipe with a plunger and a nail for a firing pin. The trap gun was designed to fire a single shotgun shell upward into an invader when the tripwire was pushed forward. A man walking upright would hit the wire at ankle level.

Steve Caine had seen such booby traps before. He'd even set up a few similar devices in the past. The merc drew his survival knife from its sheath and carefully severed the wire at the trigger mechanism of the pipe gun. He made a mental note to warn the others to watch out for such contraptions.

Caine moved to more solid cover and inspected the rest of the enemy camp. Three large metal trash cans stood behind one tent. Since the group of El Dorado thugs under Weisal's command didn't seem to be directly involved in processing cocaine, the trash cans suggested the tent was probably the camp mess hall. The *coquito* slavers must have intended to spend a lot of time in the field. That meant they had lots of supplies. In fact, they had probably hauled more food, water, petrol, and assorted creature comforts in their vehicles than weapons and ammunition.

Steve Caine smiled thinly. The *coquitos* didn't seem to be terribly fond of roughing it. Most of them were probably city-raised lowlife, men more at home with concrete walls than forests. Caine also came from a city background, but he had spent half his life learning and perfecting survival skills in jungles and forests. The *coquitos* were out of their regular environment. They had ventured into a realm where Steve Caine felt most at home, like a leopard that stalks its prey in the dark.

Caine located the diesel generators and discovered a number of gasoline tanks loaded in the back of a deuce-and-a-half truck. The enemy fuel supply. Only two sentries walked patrol around the edge of the base and neither seemed very concerned about the possibility the camp might be attacked. After all, the government hadn't been able to put a dent in El Dorado. Who would dare attack them? Caine was eager to show them the answer to that question.

Nothing Caine discovered surprised him much until he noticed the red banner hanging from the mouth of a tent located near the abandoned mine shaft. The scarlet flag had a large white circle with a black swastika in the center. Caine was startled by the Nazi banner, although he recalled the villagers' claim that Erik Weisal was the son of a Nazi war criminal.

Caine returned quietly to O'Neal's position and told the Hard Corps leader what he'd found. O'Neal allowed Caine to guide him from point to point through the forest. If Caine figured it was too risky for both men to move to a position, O'Neal followed his judgment. O'Neal got to see most of the enemy camp for himself and he knew he could trust Caine's information regarding the rest.

O'Neal and Caine finally regrouped with Fanelli and Murphy. James Wentworth and Victor Garcia were also waiting for them. The Hard Corps commander explained the setup to the other men.

"Okay," O'Neal continued. "We've got some prime targets to deal with. We want to take out the generators to plunge them suddenly in darkness. That'll help disorient and confuse the sons of bitches. We also want to make certain they don't get to those vehicles. Joe, I think you can take care of that."

"Boom," Fanelli said with a grin.

"Thought you'd like that," O'Neal remarked. "Steve, you can take out the guards and the generators. I don't have to give you any advice about the former and I figure putting the generators out of order will be easy enough."

"A couple of fistfuls of dirt in the fuel tanks ought to do it," Caine said with a nod.

"The rest of us will get into position and pretty much play it by ear," O'Neal continued. "Now, remember the Indians in our group aren't experienced combat vets. Try to keep them in low-risk duties and remind them not to shoot at anyone unless they're sure of the target. None of us want to get shot by friendly fire.''

"And watch out for booby traps," Caine added. ''I disconnected one trap gun and they've probably got more of them posted around here. Might have some other type of booby traps as well. If I was setting up traps for this area, I think I'd favor variations of animal snares and maybe a couple of punji foot holes.''

"What's that?" Garcia inquired.

"Shallow hole covered with grass or loose brush," Caine answered. "Person steps in it and his foot is trapped in a small pit with punji sticks jutting in all directions. Can't pull your leg free without nearly tearing your foot off in the process. If the tips of the punji sticks have been dipped in shit, then you'll have a nasty case of blood poisoning as well.''

"I'm sorry I asked," Garcia admitted. He took a small piece of paper from a pocket and handed it to O'Neal. "You'd better take this. Might need it."

"What is it?" O'Neal asked, looking at the numbers on the paper and a single word, *fisherman*, written on the sheet.

"That's a telephone number in La Paz to contact my CIA connection," Garcia explained. "The other numbers are a radio frequency in case you can't use a phone. 'Fisherman' is the code name so they'll know who you are. Figured you should have that in case I don't make it."

"You'd better make it," O'Neal declared with mock gruffness. He slipped the note into a shirt pocket. "I hate to talk to those sneaky-pete assholes.''

"We're pretty low on ammo, Bill," Wentworth reminded O'Neal. "And I don't think that's going to be a problem for El Dorado."

"We'll have to make our ammunition count," O'Neal answered. "Try to conserve ammo and use knives, clubs— whatever, if possible. The enemy probably has lots of extra rounds, but most of them aren't carrying spare magazines for their weapons. That means they'll have to get more ammo from their tents. If they can't get in the tents, that'll solve our problem.''

"How do we manage that?" Murphy asked. "Run over and sew the openings to the tents shut?"

"Don't be silly," O'Neal said with a shrug. "We'll just make things a little too hot for them to handle.''

CHAPTER 17

STEVE CAINE LURKED silently in the bushes surrounding the enemy camp. He had returned to a position at the outskirts of the base in order to observe the *coquitos* as he waited for the opportunity to take action. He didn't have to wait long.

The commotion within the camp had tapered off. Many of the *coquitos* had retired into the tents used as billets. Others were clustered around a campfire at the center of the camp. Three higher-ranking El Dorado thugs had been called into Erik Weisal's command tent, no doubt to discuss strategy.

The situation appeared to be about as favorable as it was apt to get. The enemy were preoccupied with each other and didn't suspect trouble. The two sentries continued to patrol the edge of the campsite, repeating a monotonous routine again and again. Neither guard was very alert and both occasionally marched beyond the view of the *coquitos* at the center of the camp.

Caine stalked his first quarry. The guard had walked toward the motor pool, whistling softly as if he'd decided to entertain himself. Caine moved to the edge of the camp and crouched behind a tree trunk. The sentry passed him without even glancing at the tree.

The mercenary drew his survival knife and crept forward on the balls of his feet. He attacked the sentry from behind. Caine's left hand closed around the man's mouth and pulled him back as the right arm swung the knife in an overhand grip. Caine plunged the six-inch blade into his opponent's heart. The sentry's scream was muffled by Caine's palm as the mercenary dragged the dying man into the brush. The merc pinned the sentry to the ground and kept his hand over the guy's mouth until the body stopped twitching. Certain the guard was dead, Caine grabbed the knife handle and worked it to and fro until the blade slid from the sentry's lifeless flesh.

Caine used the dead man's clothes to wipe blood off his hands. He retrieved his MAT-49 submachine gun, bow, and quiver of arrows. The merc knelt by the tree trunk and scanned the campsite, searching for the other sentry. He couldn't find the son of a bitch.

The second sentry hadn't noticed that his partner was missing because he had stepped outside the edge of the camp at the east side. The guard unslung an FAL assault rifle from his shoulder and braced it against the side of a tree. He unbuttoned the fly to his trousers and prepared to relieve himself, aiming at the base of the tree.

Victor Garcia emerged from a hiding place behind some bushes near the sentry's position. The big DEA agent crept behind the *coquito* as the sound of splashing urine helped conceal his footfalls. Garcia raised a hand and thrust the heel of his palm into the base of the guard's skull.

The blow slammed the sentry's face into the tree trunk. The man groaned as his forehead smashed against the hard surface. Garcia grabbed his opponent's hair and rammed the *coquito*'s face into the tree twice more to be certain the man was either unconscious or dead before he dragged the thug into the bush.

Joe Fanelli and Paddy Murphy sneaked into the enemy base, creeping behind the column of vehicles in the motor pool. Fanelli opened his canvas sack and removed the tin cans and bottles that contained the makeshift explosives he had nicknamed "holy bat shit" in honor of the main ingredient used for the unorthodox compound.

He placed the bombs, one by one, under the trucks and Jeeps. Fanelli put the charges directly beneath the fuel tanks and extended the fuses beyond each vehicle. Murphy barely glanced at Fanelli as he removed petrol cans from the back of the deuce-and-a-half that the *coquitos* used as a storage center.

The Irish gunrunner carried the fuel into the forest and returned for another load. Each can weighed ten liters and Murphy didn't care to get a hernia trying to carry more than two cans at a time. Fanelli had finished setting the explosives as Murphy hauled two more cans from the deuce-and-a-half.

Voices startled the pair. Two *coquitos* had decided to examine the pickup truck and Jeep, which had returned from the village in rather wretched condition. The pair might have been mechanics who would have to try to repair the vehicles. Fanelli overheard one of the men hiss "*Cristo*" as he inspected the ruptured radiator of the pickup.

Murphy put down the gas cans. The containers tapped together with a harsh metallic ring. The Irishman sucked in his breath with a pained expression on his face. Fanelli knelt behind the deuce-and-a-half, drew his Browning pistol, and hoped the *coquitos* hadn't heard the noise.

"*¿Qué es esto?*" one of the Bolivian thugs remarked, dashing the mercenary's hopes.

The two goons headed toward the sound. One man held an Ingram MAC-10 in his fists while his partner drew a machete from a belt sheath. They stepped to the rear of the deuce-and-a-half. The two gas cans stood in plain view, but Fanelli and Murphy had vanished. The *coquitos* slowly approached, glancing about in search of whoever had removed the cans from the truck. Neither man noticed Joe Fanelli, crawling under the rig to the opposite side of the truck. He climbed to his feet and pointed the Browning in their direction.

"*¿Quién es?*" he called softly, asking who was there.

The two El Dorado thugs assumed that the voice belonged to one of their comrades. They turned to face Fanelli and stared into the black muzzle of the merc's pistol. Taken off-guard, the pair froze, unsure what to do.

Their backs were turned to Paddy Murphy as the gun-runner stepped from behind the truck and drew a stout club from his belt. The Irishman had made the cudgel from a heavy oak branch with a thick, knobby end. He swung the club with all his might and hit the nearest *coquito* in the back of the skull.

The man collapsed to the ground. His alarmed partner stared down at him. Fanelli stepped forward suddenly and slammed the frame of his Browning across the guy's face. The *coquito* moaned as he landed on his back and tried to raise his machete. Fanelli pinned the man's wrist to the ground with a boot and hammered the butt of his pistol between the hoodlum's eyes.

Murphy clubbed his opponent again to make certain he wouldn't get up. Fanelli dragged the other unconscious thug behind the truck. Murphy gathered up the gas cans and headed for the trees. The Hard Corps demolitions expert grabbed two more containers from the truck and opened one can to pour a trail of gasoline along the rear of the vehicles, making certain the fuel touched the fuses of the "holy bat shit" bombs beneath the Jeeps and trucks.

Fanelli closed the can and followed Murphy into the forest. William O'Neal was waiting for them. The Hard Corps leader helped carry the gasoline to a safe area roughly two hundred yards from the campsite. They had decided to steal enough fuel for the Chevy to drive across Bolivia to the border of a neighboring country. They had

considered stealing one of the enemy vehicles, but the risk
was too great.

"When the hell are we going to hit these bastards?"
Murphy asked in a tense whisper.

"When the lights go out," O'Neal replied.

Steve Caine was in the process of taking care of that
part of the plan. He had crept to the generators and un-
screwed the lids to the diesel fuel tanks. He scooped up a
fistful of dirt and poured it into the opening of a tank.
Caine repeated the procedure until he'd put two fist-sized
clods of dirt into each generator. The motors soon began to
sputter as the dirt clogged the fuel lines.

Caine hurried into the forest and joined O'Neal, Fanelli,
and Murphy. The lights throughout the enemy base began
to flicker and soon went out altogether. Fanelli handed
Caine a damp strip of canvas. The cloth reeked of gasoline. Caine tied the strip to the end of an arrow and
notched it to the string of his bow. Fanelli opened a Zippo
lighter and sparked the flame to life.

"Shoot it into the stream of gasoline at the rear of the
trucks," he told Caine. "The bat-shit bombs will do the
rest."

"I hope so," Caine replied as Fanelli set fire to the rag
tied to the end of the arrow.

The camp was filled with alarmed voices and figures
scrambling about in the dark. Several flashlight beams
swung in different directions. Virtually all the *coquitos* had
emerged from the tents and were now clustered in the
center of the camp. Erik Weisal, Ramon Delgadillo, and a
couple of the lesser lieutenants yelled at their henchmen,
telling them to shut up and calm down.

Caine drew back the bowstring, aiming more by instinct
than sight because the flaming arrow head distorted his
vision. He launched the arrow quickly, aware that hesita-
tion wouldn't improve the odds of hitting the target and the
fiery arrow might start to burn his bow if he waited too

long. The missile sailed through the darkness like a miniature comet. It landed in the motor pool near the column of vehicles. Flames ignited the stream of gasoline immediately and fire streaked across the motor pool.

The blaze reached the fuses of Fanelli's bat-shit bombs. The charges went off almost simultaneously. The multiple explosions erupted into a single monstrous roar. Trucks and Jeeps burst apart and sent showers of metal and flaming debris in all directions. Some of the shrapnel descended among *coquitos* who'd ventured toward the motor pool after the generators went dead. These individuals immediately had a great deal in common with the inoperative diesel motors.

Sharp steel shards slashed into flesh, powered by the force of the explosions. The projectiles struck like bullets and cut like flying razors. Three Bolivian thugs were instantly killed by the wave of metallic hailstones. Two others weren't as lucky. They collapsed to the ground, screaming in agony as blood poured from torn flesh and punctured eyeballs.

"Looks as if the party's started," James Wentworth remarked as he watched the explosions and flames turn the motor pool into an inferno. "Let's not be wallflowers, gentlemen."

"You said it," Victor Garcia agreed. He turned to the Aymara Indians in their team. "*¡Asalto, compañeros! ¡Asalto!*"

Raul Metza and his fellow villagers charged toward the enemy base, led by Wentworth and Garcia. Four members of the second attack force hurled Molotov cocktails at the tents. The kerosene-filled bottle bombs exploded and dosed the canvas walls with flaming liquid. The tents were rapidly shrouded in fire.

One of the Aymara recruits failed to notice the trip wire of a trap gun. His ankle pushed the wire and triggered a pipe gun. The shotgun shell blasted a load of buckshot from the crude barrel and smashed pellets into the torso of the Indian. Skin, muscle, and bone gave way under the multiple projectiles. Heart and lungs crushed by the blast, the man was dead before he hit the ground.

The surviving members of the strike team had more to fear from the *coquito* gunmen than any booby traps that might remain. El Dorado henchmen opened fire with weapons switched to full-auto, spraying bullets wildly although they had no definite targets. Wentworth dove to the ground and the men in his team followed his example.

"Hold your fire, you idiots!" Weisal shouted in Spanish.

No one seemed to notice the order. The gunmen continued to blast away at the forest as if they had an unlimited supply of ammunition. However, the tents continued to burn, cutting off their access to any extra rounds kept in the shelters.

Steve Caine helped to make this situation even worse. He launched another flaming arrow into Weisal's command tent. One of the German's lieutenants headed for the tent to try to put out the blaze. Paddy Murphy followed the guy's progress through the sights of his M-16 assault rifle and fired a three-round burst. The trio of 5.56-mm slugs penetrated between the *coquito*'s seventh and eighth vertebra, severing the spinal cord and dropping the man in his tracks.

More gunfire cut down several other El Dorado hoodlums. Wentworth and Garcia fired their weapons into a group of *coquitos* who'd stupidly bunched into a tight formation. The high-velocity slugs tore clear through men's torsos and smashed into other thugs before coming to a halt. The group slumped to the ground, corpses leaning against corpses.

Weisal's men scrambled in all directions to try to escape the carnage, but O'Neal's men cut them off at the west while Wentworth's team held the east. Bullets slammed into enemy gunmen and sent their bodies toppling into the

dust. Few ventured toward the fiery remains of the motor
pool, which seemed to be a solid wall of flame.

Those bold souls who dared approach the hellish barri-
cade discovered there was no escape there either. Steve
Caine took out one bold *coquito* with a well-placed arrow
that skewered the man's neck like a shish kebab. Blood
gushed from severed carotids as the man dropped to his
knees, fists tugging at the ends of the arrow, which jutted
from each side of his neck.

Two of his comrades turned sharply and fired in the
general direction where they thought the unseen archer
lurked. Bullets raked the trees and bushes near Caine's
position, but none of the rounds came closer than two feet
from the intended target. Caine notched another arrow to
the bowstring, pulled it back, and launched the missile into
the stomach of one of the gunmen.

The hood doubled up with a bansheelike howl, but his
partner was now positive of Caine's location. He emptied
the magazine of his Heckler & Koch MP-5 into the bushes
where he suspected the bowman was hidden. In fact, the
site *had* been Caine's position, but the cunning merc had
already abandoned the spot to move behind the trunk of a
tree.

Caine had also left his bow and arrows when he changed
positions. He decided the silent long-range weapon had
served its purpose, yet the bow required longer to load
and fire than the MAT-49 submachine gun he carried.
Caine unslung the French chatterbox from his shoulder as
the *coquito* gunsel discarded his empty H&K and drew a
pistol from shoulder leather.

The dumb bastard figured he'd either hit Caine or the
archer had run out of arrows. His simpleminded logic
dictated that a man wouldn't use a bow and arrows if he
had a gun. Caine showed the man how wrong he was. The
merc aimed his MAT-49 around the edge of the tree trunk
and opened fire. Three 7.62-mm slugs tore into the enemy

gunman's chest. The thug was almost too astonished to feel pain. Then he felt nothing except the cold final grip of death.

Raul Metza noticed two El Dorado cockroaches had dashed inside a tent that had yet to receive any fiery projectiles. The Indian youth struck a match, lit the rag stuffed into the mouth of another Molotov, and hurled the bottle into the opening of the tent. Flames erupted inside the canvas structure.

One of the *coquitos* charged from the tent, his shirt and hair covered with hungry, dancing flames. He shrieked in agony as he staggered across the heart of the campsite. Horrified thugs bolted from the blazing apparition. The burning figure stumbled and fell face first to the ground. Another Aymara warrior took pity on the charred *coquito*. He fired half a dozen AK-47 rounds into the barbecued body to end the man's suffering.

The Indian's act of mercy cost him his own life. The muzzle flash of his weapon betrayed his location to a pair of El Dorado triggermen. They blasted the area with automatic fire. Bullets smashed a diagonal line across the Indian's chest and burst his heart like a bubble struck by a BB pellet.

The two gunmen didn't live long enough to congratulate themselves on their marksmanship. William O'Neal had seen the pair waste one of the men under his command. The Hard Corps leader raised his Uzi, his rage controlled by the icy discipline developed by years of training and combat experience. O'Neal opened fire and pumped three 9-mm rounds into his opponents. Two bullets scored a double hit in the center of a *coquito*'s chest while the third round caught his partner at the bridge of the nose.

Erik Weisal fired his Walther P-38 at the muzzle flash of the attackers' weapons, but he realized the effort was in vain. Most of the enemy were out of pistol range and the others were sheltered by carefully selected cover. The invaders were good, Weisal realized, very good.

"They've got us surrounded," Delgadillo remarked, ducking low to avoid a flaming strip of canvas as the tent burned. "Any ideas, jefe?"

Weisal glanced up at the Nazi flag. The banner was shrouded in flames. The fire consumed the fabric rapidly. The swastika vanished within the blaze and the blackened remnants dangled from the charred flagpole. Weisal's stomach knotted with anger and sorrow as he watched the banner of his father's beloved Third Reich reduced to glowing ashes.

"Jefe?" Delgadillo insisted. The Bolivian didn't give a damn about the Nazi flag. The Third Reich was as dead as Adolf Hitler and only a handful of fanatics would want to revive it. Delgadillo was more concerned about personal survival at the moment. "What should we do?"

"We retreat to the mine," Weisal declared, looking away from the burned flag. "There's a cache of weapons stored there. Machine guns, assault rifles, crates of ammunition."

"If we all try to flee to the cave half our forces will be cut down before we can reach shelter," Delgadillo stated. "The enemy won't be foolish enough to rush our position if we make it to the mine. If there are enough of them—"

"Quiet!" Weisal said sharply. He hadn't remained at the top of El Dorado's dung heap for more than a decade without being able to make decisions quickly and ruthlessly. "We'll take three men to help us with the weapons. The rest will continue to fight the enemy."

"Use them for cannon fodder?" Delgadillo was startled by Weisal's willingness to sacrifice his own men in such a ruthless manner. "But they've been loyal to us . . ."

"Then they can prove their loyalty by keeping our enemies occupied while we make a strategic withdrawal!" Weisal replied savagely. "I don't have time to argue with

you, Ramon. I'm taking four men to the mine. Do you
want to survive or do you choose to take your chances
with the others in the open?''

''Who will the other three men be, jefe?'' Delgadillo
asked in a voice made small by the pressure of shame.

''Choose three men at random,'' the German gangster
answered. He noticed a trio of *coquitos* crouched on the
ground, trying to shoot at the all-but-invisible attackers
beyond the limits of the base. ''They'll do. Just tell them
to follow you and bring them here immediately.''

''*Sí*, jefe,'' the Bolivian answered with a sigh.

The gun battle continued to rage as Weisal and his chosen
few ducked into the mouth of the abandoned mine shaft.
The Hard Corps team and the *coquito* henchmen were too
busy staying alive and trying to kill each other to notice
five men running into the hole in the mountainside. Victor
Garcia saw the last two lieutenants about to disappear inside the mine. He quickly aimed his AK-47 at the pair and
fired the last of his 7.62-mm ammo. Three bullets sparked
against the rock wall surrounding the entrance. Another
bullet smashed into the back of an opponent and sent the thug
tumbling down the hill.

The fierce shooting contest came to an end. The ground
was covered with the corpses of more than thirty slain El
Dorado hoodlums. Since the Hard Corps had cut off their
avenues of escape and destroyed the enemy's cover, the
only advantage the *coquitos* had was sheer numbers. Their
ranks had been sharply reduced; only eight of the Bolivian
thugs remained.

The *coquitos* had exhausted their ammunition, but their
machismo refused to allow them to surrender. Some of the
survivors drew machetes or hunting knives. Others grabbed
the barrels of empty rifles and subguns and held them like
clubs.

The Hard Corps strike force was in a similar condition.

They had also burned up all the ammo for their rifles and
submachine guns. Only their Browning pistols remained
loaded and they had precious little 9-mm ammo left.

"You fockin' gringo sk-um *sacos*!" a thug with a limited command of English snarled at the forest. "Come
fight face lookin' at face!"

William O'Neal marched from the forest. He lowered
his Uzi to the ground and drew a machete from its belt
sheath. Fanelli and Caine appeared behind the merc commander. O'Neal pointed his jungle knife at the *coquito*
who'd issued the challenge.

"You got it, fella," O'Neal announced.

The Bolivian hoodlum snarled an obscenity and raised
his own machete. O'Neal waited for the thug to make the
first move. The *coquito* didn't disappoint him. The hoodlum's jungle knife swung a short feint and quickly swooped
into a cross-body cut aimed at O'Neal's head.

The Hard Corps leader blocked the knife swing with the
blade of his own machete and launched a karate snap-kick
to the *coquito*'s gut. The thug groaned and folded at the
middle. O'Neal's left hand streaked out and seized his
opponent's elbow to push the enemy's machete arm farther
away.

O'Neal raised his own knife and swung the weapon.
The heavy blade chopped through the *coquito*'s forehead
and sharp steel bit into brain matter. Blood flowed from
the horrible wound and crimson streamed down his face.
O'Neal grabbed the handle of the machete with both hands
and yanked the blade from the dead man's split skull.

Another *coquito* immediately attacked O'Neal, swinging
the stock of an empty FAL rifle at the merc's head.
O'Neal blocked with the machete blade. Steel rang against
steel less than an inch from his right ear. O'Neal pushed
the guy's weapon back with the machete blade and slashed
at his opponent's belly.

The thug jumped back to avoid the knife stroke and

swung his rifle. The machete missed its target and the *coquito*'s improvised club chopped the jungle knife hard enough to wrench the machete from O'Neal's grasp. The hood swung the rifle in a rising sweep for O'Neal's face, but the merc dodged the attack. The *coquito* slashed another butt stroke at O'Neal's skull, hoping to take the Hard Corps leader's head off with the force of the blow.

O'Neal ducked under the sweeping gun stock. He lunged forward and rammed his skull into the *coquito*'s breadbasket and quickly grabbed his opponent's ankles. O'Neal yanked hard and pulled the man's feet out from under him. The *coquito* crashed on his back with a gasp as air was forced from his lungs. O'Neal stamped a bootheel between the thug's legs, stomping the guy's testicles to a pulp. The man uttered a single, high-pitched shriek and fainted.

Two other El Dorado flunkies attacked Fanelli and Caine. Joe Fanelli held his empty MAT-49 in one hand and knelt to scoop up some dirt with his other hand. A machete-wielding lunatic charged at Fanelli, jungle knife raised overhead. The Italian-American merc hurled the dirt in his opponent's face and sidestepped the awkward machete stroke when the blinded hoodlum angrily slashed at the blurred target.

"A lot of dust in the air, ain't there?" Fanelli remarked as he slammed the MAT-49 across his opponent's wrists to strike the machete from the man's fingers.

Spitting dirt from his mouth and still half-blind from crud in his eyes, the angry *coquito* swung a wild left hook at Fanelli. His fist connected with the frame of the merc's French subgun. The man howled as he staggered away, nursing his left hand in his right. He had broken two knuckles.

Fanelli turned slightly and rammed the metal stock of the MAT-49 into the guy's solar plexus. The goon doubled up with a choking gasp and Fanelli stamped the butt of his submachine gun into the seventh vertebra at the base of his opponent's neck. Bone cracked and the man fell on his face, his neck broken.

Steve Caine faced a *coquito* armed with an empty M-16 rifle, which he swung like a club at the mercenary's head. Caine met the charge with an improvised spear he had made by fitting a four-foot-pole into the hollow handle of his survival knife and tying the hilt securely into place with fishing line.

Caine raised the shaft of his weapon to block the thug's clumsy attack and quickly delivered a butt stroke to his opponent's face. The *coquito* staggered backward, but managed to keep his balance and lunged with the barrel of his rifle, planning to rip open Caine from crotch to navel with the sharp front sight of the weapon.

The mercenary dodged the attack and thrust his spear, driving the knife blade under the hood's breastbone. Six inches of sharp steel carved upward to fillet the heart and lungs. The *coquito* opened his mouth and vomited blood across the front of his shirt. His body went limp and Caine lowered the dead weight to the ground, placed a foot on the corpse, and yanked the blade from the lifeless lump, which had formerly been a man.

The remaining four survivors among the *coquito* henchmen had turned to the west side to discover Wentworth, Garcia, and Raul were waiting for them. James Wentworth held his cavalry saber in a two-hand grip. Victor Garcia drew a machete from his belt and Raul carried an improvised club.

"Come on, you maggots," Wentworth told the hoodlums. "Let's finish this nonsense so we can go home."

Two *coquitos* attacked Wentworth. One man raised a rifle overhead like a club while the other wielded a hatchet. Wentworth stepped forward and swung his saber, his entire body moving in unison to deliver the *kenjutsu* sword stroke. The long steel blade cut a fast arc to meet the first opponent's rifle.

The saber struck the hoodlum's left wrist, slicing through muscle and bone. The *coquito* screamed as blood bubbled from severed arteries in his wrist. His sliced hand was still fisted around the barrel of the rifle. As the wounded man staggered forward and fell to his knees the second attacker swung his hatchet at Wentworth.

The *kenjutsu*-trained mercenary swiftly jumped backward to avoid the deadly sweep of the hatchet blade. The saber gave Wentworth superior reach and he immediately took advantage of this by delivering a quick sword thrust. The steel tip pierced the hollow of his opponent's throat. Blood seeped from the wound as the *coquito*'s eyes and mouth opened wide in mute terror. The man realized he was about to die. Wentworth turned his wrists sharply and sliced the blade through the side of his opponent's neck to free the saber. The man collapsed as crimson drenched his shirt.

Wentworth sensed danger from behind and glimpsed a machete-wielding adversary about to chop a jungle knife across the back of his neck. The merc stepped forward and swung the saber blade overhead, extending it across his back to protect his neck from the machete stroke. Steel rang sourly against steel as the blades met.

Wentworth whirled, pivoting on one foot and slashing a cross-body sword stroke, cutting with the motion of his body. The saber caught the machete man across the abdomen. The hoodlum cried out as sharp steel carved into his bowels. He dropped his machete and staggered backward, both hands clutching his wounded belly. Wentworth followed with another sword stroke to the side of his opponent's neck and severed the carotid artery and jugular vein with a single cut.

The man sank to the ground, more dead than alive. Wentworth turned to find the fourth and last *coquito* locked in combat with Victor Garcia. The hoodlum had attacked Garcia with a machete and the DEA agent defended himself with an identical jungle knife. Blades clashed and both men seized the other's wrist and struggled to disarm one another.

Garcia was bigger and stronger than his opponent. He soon bent the other man backward and twisted the hood's wrist to force him to release the machete. Garcia's head snapped forward and butted the *coquito* in the face. The unexpected blow knocked the man to the ground and Garcia immediately plunged the point of his machete into the thug's chest. The jungle knife impaled the fallen *coquito* and pinned him to the ground like an insect in a specimen collection.

Wentworth heard sobbing mixed with hissing curses in ragged Spanish. He gazed down at the hoodlum he'd taken out of action by cutting off the man's hand. The wounded *coquito* held the stump of his wrist with his other hand, trying to pinch off the arteries to stop the flow of blood from the severed limb. The man would bleed to death if they didn't get him to a hospital in a hurry . . . and there weren't any hospitals for many miles.

"*Adiós,*" Wentworth muttered as he raised the saber and sailed the blade into the wounded man's neck.

"*¡Madre de Dios!*" Raul Metza gasped as he watched the thug's severed head tumble across the ground. The Indian youth stared at the decapitated corpse. "Was this necessary, señor?"

"Under the circumstances," Wentworth replied, flicking blood from the blade of his saber, "it was merciful."

CHAPTER 18

"MISSION ACCOMPLISHED, GENTLEMEN," William O'Neal announced. He smiled at Garcia. "You want me to return that note with the code name and the numbers now?"

"Keep it," the DEA agent replied, gazing up at the mine shaft. He was about to speak, but O'Neal turned and shouted orders to his men.

"Joe! Steve! Get around that fire and spray it down with the extinguishers before it spreads into the forest!" the Hard Corps leader commanded. "Get Murphy to give you a hand. Where the hell is that Irish bastard?"

"Two of our Indian friends were killed," Wentworth told O'Neal. "Raul and a villager named Angelo are okay. All things considered, we came out of this battle pretty well."

"Could have gone better, but it could have been worse," O'Neal remarked. "Tell Raul and the other guy to help put out the fire. Then you can help me check the enemy to make certain none of them are playing 'possum."

"Hey, damn it!" Garcia said sharply. "I saw Weisal and a couple of his goons head for—"

Victor Garcia convulsed suddenly as bullets ripped through his chest. The DEA agent tumbled to the ground, blood oozing from at least three bullet wounds in his upper torso.

More projectiles tore through the camp, ripping up mounds of dirt near the fleeing figures of O'Neal and Wentworth.

The mercenary officers rolled to cover behind a broad tree trunk as a wave of high-velocity rounds raked the area. The high rate of fire told O'Neal and Wentworth they were being attacked by a light machine gun.

O'Neal peered around the edge of the trunk and looked up at the mine shaft in the side of the mountain. Two figures were stationed at the mouth of the tunnel, positioned behind a black metal log mounted on a bipod. The big machine gun appeared to be a 7.62-mm M-60 or a weapon of similar design. One *coquito* fired the weapon while his partner guided the ammo belt into the chamber.

"Must've had that chopper hidden in the mine," O'Neal rasped through clenched teeth. "Hard to say what else they've got up there."

"Since we don't even have a rifle with ammo left," Wentworth muttered, "they don't need anything else. A goddamn mounted machine gun is more than enough."

"What the hell happened to that Russian rocket launcher?" O'Neal demanded. "The damn thing was in the truck when we left the village."

"It's in the forest somewhere," Wentworth answered. "One of the Indians was carrying it when he got wasted."

"Great," O'Neal muttered sourly.

Erik Weisal leaned out of the mouth of the cave, peering down at the demolished camp through the lenses of a pair of Steiner binoculars. He smiled when he spotted Garcia's still body on the ground. *One less opponent to deal with. The others will also pay with their lives*, Weisal vowed.

The enemy had gotten the better of his men by surprise attack, but now Weisal and his four men had the advantage. They had claimed the high ground and the enemy had no doubt lost many of their members in the firefight. The enemy was surely low on ammunition, while Weisal had plenty of full-auto weapons and crates of extra ammo. He could hold off any army from the mouth of the mine—or annihilate a small assault force.

There appeared to be fewer opponents than Weisal had guessed from the fury of the assault: less than a dozen men. It seemed remarkable that such a small number of opponents could have taken out his entire camp. Weisal rationalized that most of the assault force must have died during the battle.

"Over there!" he shouted when he spotted movement below. "To the left, at about two hundred meters!"

The machine gunners shifted their weapon and fired a volley of full-auto projectiles in the general direction of the destroyed motor pool where Fanelli, Caine, Raul, and Angelo were trying to put out the fire. However, the *coquito* killers weren't in a good position to aim at the four men near the flaming wreckage. Bullets slashed the area, but the Hard Corps NCOs and their Indian allies managed to reach cover before the enemy gunners could claim another victim.

"*Scheisse!*" Weisal cursed in his father's language. He switched back to Spanish. "Can't you fools hit a moving target even with a machine gun?"

"They haven't exactly had regular practice with these weapons," Delgadillo remarked as he moved along the rock walls, checking the various weapons to select a rifle for his own use during the counterattack.

Many of Weisal's weapons were American. Others were from black-market arms dealers in Argentina, Brazil, and European sources. Delgadillo was not familiar with most of these guns. He was a gangster, not a soldier. Why the hell should he need to learn how to handle a mounted machine gun? Who would have guessed something like this would happen?

"So you failed to train your men properly, Ramon?" Weisal snapped, eager to blame failure on someone other than himself. "Perhaps that's why so many of them have died this night. That's a shortcoming we'll have to correct in the future when we build up another unit to continue operations, after we've finished killing these scum!"

The *coquito* hit team turned their weapon around and delivered another murderous salvo at O'Neal and Wentworth's position. Bullets chipped bark from the oak tree they used for cover. The mercs heard slugs thud into the thick trunk. They couldn't move, but so far the enemy hadn't been able to hit them either. However, the Bolivian hoodlums could keep them pinned down with the machine gun while one or more of the gangsters moved into position to pick off the Hard Corps team with rifles or hand grenades.

"We can't stay here," O'Neal growled. "But moving won't be easy. Doubt if we'll get two yards before the bastards cut us down."

"That's not very encouraging, Bill," Wentworth remarked. He gasped as a bullet ricochet whined past his left ear. "Maybe their weapon will jam or they'll run out of ammo . . ."

"Maybe they'll both have a fuckin' heart attack," O'Neal snorted. "Our best chance is to wait for the gunners to swing their weapon away from us and make a run for it."

"Nice idea," Wentworth said dryly. "Where are we gonna run to?"

Suddenly a large projectile burst from the tree line. It streaked across the night sky and sailed toward the mine shaft. The machine gunners saw the missile a split second before it struck. A single scream of fear shrieked into the predawn sky an instant before the rocket exploded. The blast smashed the machine gun and hurled it off the mountain side. Chunks of human remains mingled with the debris.

"*Nein!*" Weisal shouted as the lumber supports of the entrance to the mine gave way.

More than a ton of rock crashed down across the mouth of the tunnel. Weisal shouted in rage and terror as he staggered away from the falling boulders. Ramon Delgadillo crossed himself and muttered a half-remembered prayer before a loose rock hit him between the shoulder blades and drove him to his knees.

Weisal's raving changed to a furious song of defiance. He managed to sing the first line of the *Horst Wessel Lied* before his mouth and throat filled with rock dust. Choking, he stumbled farther inside the mine shaft. A loose beam had fallen in his path. Half-blind, the Nazi tripped over the obstacle and fell face-first to the stone floor as more rocks continued to cave in all around him.

The entire mouth of the cave was soon covered with rubble. A cloud of dust billowed among the stony ruins, like a fog drifting across the face of a tombstone. The mountain was finally quiet. Not even a whimper escaped the sealed entrance of the mine.

"Look what I found!" Paddy Murphy called out as he emerged from the forest with the Soviet-made RPG-7 rocket launcher propped across his shoulder. "And not a bloody moment too soon."

"Good work, Murphy!" O'Neal replied, stepping from the tree. "We wondered what happened to you. Afraid you might have bought the farm."

"Just puttering about in the woods," the Irishman explained as he lowered the launcher and gazed up at his handiwork. "Looks like Erik Weisal and his blokes are finished."

"Thanks to you," O'Neal said with a nod.

Wentworth hurried to the fallen figure of Victor Garcia. He doubted that the DEA agent had survived being drilled by three or more 7.62-mm bullets, but he checked for a pulse anyway. The Hard Corps lieutenant uttered a sigh when he failed to find any trace of life. Garcia's eyes gazed up in the frozen expression of death. Wentworth placed two fingers on Garcia's eyelids and eased them shut.

The Hard Corps and their allies eventually extinguished the fire and covered the smoldering remains with dirt. The air was pungent with the scent of burned gunpowder, charred human flesh, and the strong odor of fresh blood. The aftermath of the battle was horrific with mangled, dismembered bodies scattered across the grounds.

"I didn't know it would be like this," Raul whispered, staring at the terrible remnants of the battle. "How can you stand to do this over and over again? How can you stand to look at it afterward?"

"A man does what he's good at," O'Neal said with a shrug, although he realized this was a pretty poor excuse. In truth, O'Neal didn't know the answer.

"Captain," Fanelli began as he approached. "What do you want to do with Victor's body?"

"We'll have to leave it," O'Neal answered. "DEA and CIA will take care of the details when Garcia's body is identified by whoever finds this mess."

"Señor," Angelo said, deep concern in his voice. "You cannnot ask us to leave the bodies of our dead in this terrible place. We must take them back to the village for a proper burial."

"If you and Raul want to take the bodies of your friends back to the village, that's up to you," O'Neal answered. "But you'll have to manage hauling them back to the truck without our help. We've got six cans of gasoline, a rocket launcher, and whatever else we can salvage from the dead, which we might need later."

"You'd steal from the dead?" Angelo glared at the merc leader.

"These El Dorado assholes were scum when they were alive and I don't see any reason to respect them now that they're dead," O'Neal stated. "We're soldiers, fella. Soldiers have to put the needs of the living above the social 'niceties commonly shown to the dead. After all, a bunch of corpses don't need weapons, ammunition, money, food, or supplies. We might need all of the above.''

"Your attitude is appalling, señor," Angelo declared, frowning.

"Tough shit," O'Neal said gruffly. "I'm tired and I'm not going to wear myself out hauling dead bodies around. Nor am I going to permit my men to exhaust themselves for a reason that isn't necessary—for us anyway. I already told you that you two can drag those corpses more than a mile to the Chevy, if you want. If it means that much to you, you'll do it. Otherwise, shut the fuck up."

"Angelo," Raul said to his fellow Aymara villager, "let us make two litters to take back the bodies of our people to their families. The captain is responsible for the welfare of his people just as we feel a responsibility for ours. Do not lecture him about morality. After all, we hired these men to help us fight El Dorado. They've upheld their honor and kept their word to us. We have no right to criticize them."

The Hard Corps and Paddy Murphy gathered up what supplies they could find among the ruins. They found several submachine guns that were still in good condition and enough 9-mm ammo to load a magazine for each weapon. O'Neal had chosen to retrieve his Uzi. Fanelli and Caine discarded their MAT-49 subguns and loaded up smaller, easier-to-conceal MAC-10 machine pistols instead. Wentworth and Murphy took Uzis from the slain *coquitos*. They also confiscated more than a hundred thousand Bolivian pesos and several hundred American dollars from the dead men.

"What's the money for?" Raul asked, obviously disappointed that the mercenaries had taken cash from the dead.

"We might need it to bribe officials or pay for repairs on the truck before we can reach the border," Wentworth explained. "Our own funds have been running out fast. We might even have to buy another new wardrobe before we leave the country."

Twenty minutes later, the Hard Corps unit was ready to pull out. Raul and Angelo had strapped the bodies of the two dead Indians into drag-litters and hauled the corpses through the forest. The Hard Corps and Murphy carried their weapons and each man hauled a can of gasoline. They had decided to leave the sixth can behind.

"You know," Murphy began as he shifted the shoulder strap of the Uzi to lean the RPG-7 against the same shoulder, "I could probably sell these guns for a nice hunk of change in La Paz."

"Too risky," O'Neal replied. "We only took the weapons in case we need them before we reach the border. When we're sure we're safe, the guns will have to be disassembled and dumped in some garbage cans or buried somewhere."

"Pity," Murphy said with a heartfelt sigh. "Well, I guess I'll be able to get into some interesting line of work when we get to the States. You blokes know anybody in the arms-dealing business?"

"Does the pope know anybody in the Vatican?" Fanelli replied with a chuckle. "We know people involved in gunrunning in six or seven countries. We even know some guys who do it legal."

"Legal?" Murphy said with a grin. "Well, maybe I'll give that a try. Might be nice for a change."

Steve Caine suddenly stiffened when he noticed a wide, square object partially concealed by bushes about a hundred yards from the path. Sunlight gleamed across Plexiglas between the branches. Two heads moved behind the transparent shield.

"Down!" Caine shouted as he hurled himself to the ground and rolled to cover behind a boulder.

O'Neal and Wentworth had seen the mysterious shape a

moment before Caine shouted his warning. They ducked for cover an instant before a stream of automatic fire erupted. The muzzle flash of a weapon appeared from the metal wall of the shape. Fanelli dropped to the ground, but a bullet raked his left shoulder blade. The tough guy from Jersey ground his teeth together as a burning pain raced through his back. He crawled to shelter behind a tree.

Murphy groaned and spun about from a bullet that punched clean through his upper arm and tore the rocket launcher from his grasp. Another bullet drilled into his left hip before he managed to drop and drag himself to cover behind a tree stump.

Raul let go of his litter and abandoned the dead man he'd been hauling across the pathway. The Indian youth jumped for shelter, but a projectile smashed into his right thigh just above the knee cap. Raul cried out and hit the ground hard. He rolled to an oak tree and stretched out behind it.

Angelo wasn't quick enough. Two 7.62-mm slugs crashed into his back and pitched him face-first to the ground between the two litters containing the dead Aymara warriors. The ambusher's weapon sprayed the fallen Indian with another salvo of full-auto rounds. Bullets tore into Angelo's twitching form and punched bloodless holes in the lifeless figures strapped to the litters.

The four Hard Corps mercs quickly brought their weapons into play. Uzis and Ingrams snarled. More than a dozen 9-mm slugs struck the metal wall and Plexiglas window. A spiderweb crack appeared in a corner of the window, but the reinforced Plexiglas held and the armored wall beneath it didn't appear even to be dented.

"Hear you my words, American shit-dogs!" Erik Weisal yelled from his steel shield as he peered through the bullet-resistant window. He only spoke a few hundred words of English and he hadn't used the language for a long time. "I kill American shit-dogs! Whores' sons! Fuck you your mothers!"

He handed a FAL assault rifle to Ramon Delgadillo. Weisal's second-in-command gave his boss a fully loaded M-16 and removed the spent magazine from the Belgium rifle. Weisal thrust the '16 through the slot in the armored wall and opened fire at the Hard Corps while Delgadillo loaded the FAL with a fresh mag.

"I thought we'd buried that bastard back in the mine shaft," Wentworth remarked, huddling behind a tree trunk that was being assaulted by a burst of 5.56-mm rounds.

"Must've been another way out of the mine," O'Neal rasped, trying to stay clear of the bullets although the stones he used for cover seemed to shift when bullets struck them. "Murphy! Load the goddamn RPG!"

"I don't have it anymore!" the Irishman replied, his voice strained as he fought to control the pain from his bullet-crushed limbs. "Son of a bitch shot it when he hit me. I think it's ruined anyway and I'm not gonna crawl out to it to find out!"

"The Plexiglas might give way if we can hit it with enough bullets," Caine suggested. He tried to point his Ingram at the enemy shield but Weisal's M-16 raked the boulder with slugs and Caine had to retreat behind his shelter.

"That Nazi bastard isn't gonna make it easy for us to aim our weapons," O'Neal commented. "If we just spray rounds at him we'll exhaust our ammo in less than a minute and still might not take out the window."

"Angelo!" Raul cried out. "I think they killed Angelo!"

"They're gonna kill all of us if we don't figure out a way to take out that modified pillbox," Fanelli shouted through clenched teeth. "I don't suppose anybody has a couple of hand grenades they've been savin' for a rainy day?"

Bullets struck one of the gas cans and punched two holes

clear through the container. There was a good chance the gasoline could be ignited by the bullets. Luckily for the Hard Corps, it didn't blow. Petrol leaked from the punctured can. The pool began to form between the pinned-down mercs.

"If a bullet sparks against a rock or something," Wentworth remarked, his voice remarkably calm, "we're going to get one hell of a nasty hot foot."

Weisal fired the last rounds from the M-16 and exchanged the empty weapon for the fully loaded FAL rifle. Ramon Delgadillo propped the '16 against the wall and pulled an old Mark I hand grenade from his belt. The Bolivian henchman yanked the pin and lobbed the grenade at the Hard Corps' position.

The explosive egg hit the ground near O'Neal and rolled downhill next to the tree stump. Paddy Murphy scrambled from cover, dragging his crippled leg, and reached for the grenade. Weisal fired his FAL and drilled two slugs into the Irishman's chest. Murphy's body jerked from the impact, but he grabbed the Mark I in his left fist and quickly hurled it back at the *coquitos'* position.

The grenade exploded, shattering the Plexiglas and driving the armored wall back into Weisal and Delgadillo. The heavy shield flattened the gangsters and pinned them to the ground.

The Hard Corps immediately rushed forward, firing their weapons as they ran. Wentworth and Fanelli sprayed Delgadillo with 9-mm slugs. The Bolivian's face vanished and his skull exploded as four parabellums reduced his head to a mass of bloody pulp.

O'Neal and Caine fired their submachine guns at Weisal. Several Uzi and Ingram rounds slammed into the German's rib cage and ripped his right arm into a bloodied slab of lifeless meat. Yet, Erik Weisal was still alive as William O'Neal approached.

"I've always wanted to kill a Nazi," the Hard Corps

commander declared as he aimed the Uzi at Weisal's forehead.

There was only one round left in the magazine.

That was all O'Neal needed to make his wish come true.

CHAPTER 19

THE HARD CORPS arrived at Chuma shortly after dusk. Chuma is a small, quiet city located near Lake Titicaca and the Peruvian border. The Chevy had overheated and they'd been forced to abandon the truck two miles outside the city limits. They had also buried the disassembled Uzis and Ingrams before entering the town. The four mercenaries still carried their Browning pistols concealed under their shirts, but they didn't really feel they'd need the guns.

They had delivered Raul and the bodies of the three slain Aymara Indians to the village. The Indians had been torn by emotions; while they grieved for their three friends, they rejoiced that Weisal and his slavers would never victimize their village again. The old man had given the Hard Corps payment for accomplishing their mission. It was four thousand Bolivian pesos—less than a hundred dollars. The Hard Corps thanked them, although they had taken far more cash from the bodies of the *coquitos*, and accepted payment. The money didn't matter, but they knew the villagers would have been insulted if they hadn't accepted it.

The Aymara gave them clean clothes, food, and water. They invited the mercenaries to stay for a celebration, which they planned to have the following day. The Hard Corps gently declined and explained that they needed to move on. The old one assured them he understood and they would always have the gratitude of the people of his village.

The Hard Corps were exhausted by the time they reached Chuma. They were also saddened by the deaths of Victor Garcia and Paddy Murphy. None of them spoke much during the trip. They had survived. Fanelli's bullet wound was only a crease, which had barely broken the skin at his shoulder blade. To still be alive and in one piece was enough to be thankful for after the experiences they'd endured since arriving in Bolivia.

William O'Neal took the note given to him by Garcia less than an hour before the DEA agent was killed in the battle at Weisal's camp. He examined the note and wondered if Garcia had somehow sensed his own death. Hell, he thought. Probably just a coincidence, another sneaky little joke Fate likes to play on you, to make you have trouble sleeping on nights when past incidents come back to haunt you.

He stepped into a public phone booth and dialed the number on the sheet of paper. A phone rang somewhere in La Paz and a CIA operative answered it.

"Yes?" a voice came on the poor connection.

"Fisherman," O'Neal replied, using Garcia's code name.

"We wondered what happened to you, Fisherman," the CIA guy stated. "Haven't heard from you for some time."

"I don't feel like dicking around on the phone, fella," O'Neal told him. "We're in Chuma and we can be in Peru within an hour. You gonna arrange transportation or do I come to La Paz and cause an incident?"

"No need to be hostile, Fisherman," the Company man stated with a sniffle. "We'll have a C-130 waiting for you along the lakeside airstrip near the border. Just cross into Peru and you'll be on your way back to the States."

"Okay," O'Neal said wearily. "Sorry I got shitty with you, but this has been a long goddamn day."

"I hope you had a pleasant stay while you were here," the guy remarked, referring to whether or not the mission succeeded.

"Could have been worse," O'Neal answered and hung up. He stepped from the phone booth and added, "Could have been better."

The Hard Corps leader shrugged. He headed across the street to tell his partners the good news.